Por   ...s, Ind.

LIFE WASN'T EASY

for Anna Elizabeth. It was not the time to dream of books and the world beyond the Brethren community to which she belonged.

Sometimes she wished she'd been born a boy, not Brethren, and certainly not a girl destined to care for home and hearth alone.

But then she remembered her family—a loving, sensible mother; an understanding father who was often too good for his rebellious daughter's comfort; and the brothers and sisters who depended on her. And her girlfriends, laughing and totally content with their spinning, churning, gossipy domestic life.

Yes, perhaps life didn't always seem fair. But Anna Elizabeth knew somehow that her very special needs would be met someday in a deeply satisfying way.

ANNA ELIZABETH

A Girl of the Plain People

LUCILE LONG

Illustrations by Inez Goughnor

THE BRETHREN PRESS ELGIN, ILLINOIS

ANNA ELIZABETH
A Girl of the Plain People

Published by Pyramid Publications for The Brethren Press

First Printing May, 1975

ISBN: 0–87178–040–2

Library of Congress Catalog Card Number: 74–29366

Copyright © 1942, 1970 by The Brethren Publishing House

All rights reserved. No part of this publication may be repro-
duced or transmitted in any form or by any means, electronic
or mechanical, including photocopy, recording, or any information storage and retrieval system, without permission in
writing from the publisher.

Printed in the United States of America

THE BRETHREN PRESS
Elgin, Illinois 60120

To
my father and mother
in whose home another little girl discovered, with a
joy as great as Anna Elizabeth's, the world of books.

FOREWORD TO THE PAPERBACK EDITION

This reprinting of *Anna Elizabeth* has been made possible partly through gifts from family and friends in memory of my husband, Harry A. Brandt, who died February 23, 1974. Perhaps it is therefore appropriate to say a few words about the book and how it came to be written.

Anna Elizabeth is historical fiction on a modest scale, with its setting in eighteenth-century Pennsylvania among the "plain people," a term that includes Brethren, Mennonites, Quakers, and other smaller sects as well. Anna Elizabeth was Brethren. This group had its beginning in Germany in 1708, but within a few decades all of the members had emigrated to Pennsylvania. Often they were called Dunkers (the German word for *dip* or *immerse* is *tunker*, and they baptize by immersion); later their official name was the German Baptist Brethren; today it is Church of the Brethren.

In this story I have used some historical characters: Christopher Sower, Maria Christina Sower, Peter Becker, Abraham Duboy, George Kline, Peter Miller, Stephen Koch, Conrad Beissel. Background details such as the comet of 1743–44 and the fair in Germantown in October are accurate. The story of Abraham Duboy's death follows that of Brumbaugh in his *History of the German Baptist Brethren*, and the stanzas from Peter Becker's hymn and the verses from the Tersteegen cards are my own metrical versions based on literal translations of the original German. From books and historical societies and museums I have learned what I could about manners and customs, dress and food for this period, and against this background I have set the story of Anna Elizabeth. My characters spoke German, of course. I have depended on inverted word order and occasional Pennsylvania Dutch phrases to suggest this.

7

Brethren interest in their beginnings began about mid-nineteenth century and developed gradually but steadily. However, although I was the daughter of a minister, a member of the church, a graduate of one of our church colleges, and a teacher in another, I had little early interest in this field. Then the summer of 1940 I worked at our church headquarters in Elgin, Illinois, and met Harry A. Brandt.

He had already spent about twenty years on the editorial staff of our church paper, the *Gospel Messenger,* and had written two books about Brethren history, *Christopher Sower and Son* and *Meet Henry Kurtz.* I had been writing for this same paper occasionally, and Mr. Brandt had been accepting my poems for publication. I found his enthusiasm about Brethren history contagious, and I had access that summer to information from the Brethren historical library and from fellow workers. And so I returned to my teaching position that fall already planning the story of Anna Elizabeth.

In the first edition (1942) I mentioned in a foreword a few of the people who had helped me in the writing of the story. I quote my concluding words: "My final word of thanks goes to Harry A. Brandt, Managing Editor of the *Gospel Messenger* and author, who first interested me in church history, who urged me to write, and who welcomed kindly this story, even though it did not follow any of his suggestions. It is largely due to his interest in Brethren literature, his encouragement, and his persistent effort that this story makes its final appearance." A little more than a quarter of a century later, when we were married, Harry A. Brandt was still interested in books, and again it was chiefly his "encouragement and persistent effort" that led to the publication of my volume of poems, *The Flame Tree* (Brethren Press, 1973).

Now *Anna Elizabeth* appears again, this time as a

memorial to a man whom I delight to honor. I dedicated the first edition to my parents. To their names I now add that of Harry A. Brandt, editor, author, publisher, long-time friend, and—last and best of all—my husband. I do this as a tribute to his lifelong love for and interest in our church, its history, good writing, and the making of books.

Lucile Long Strayer Brandt

Contents

CHAPTER I

What's in a Name?

Anna Elizabeth entered the kitchen, glanced at the cradle where her baby brother Samuel lay sleeping, and walked directly to the spinning wheel where her mother sat busily at work.

"Mother, why did not you name me Apollonia?" she asked.

Her mother stopped working the treadle for a moment in sheer astonishment.

"Why then should I name you Apollonia?" she exclaimed. "Named you are for your two grandmothers Anna and Elizabeth, and good Bible names both. Why such a question should you ask?"

Quite unabashed, Anna Elizabeth watched the spinning wheel begin again. She liked to watch her mother sit at the little wheel and spin. In fact, she liked the kitchen generally, although almost all her work was done there. To the left as one entered the kitchen door was the long table with benches on either side where they ate, and in the far corner, a cupboard for dishes.

Here the sun came in from the window between the cupboard and the table when Anna Elizabeth sat in her usual place for morning prayers. In the center of the house, of course, was the fireplace, with the bake oven at one side and a few pewter dishes on the mantel above and kettles hanging on the cranes and smaller kettles and covered iron pans around the fireplace below. On the right side was the spinning wheel, and Samuel's cradle, and the work table where food was prepared for the kettles, and another window, and the smaller movable sink where Anna Elizabeth washed dishes and pans—thousands of them, she thought sometimes. It was really a very nice kitchen, with four windows (the other two were on either side of the kitchen door) and windowpanes in them, not oiled paper at all.

"Could you have thought of the name if you had wanted to?" she persisted. "And how could Sister Lehman think to name her daughter Apollonia if you coudn't?"

Sister Landis decided to ignore this question and ask one of her own.

"Did your father get the plow fixed?"

"Yes. And Brother Hammer was there too, and his boys."

"Ah, the rain this morning kept him from the field then too. And did you ask of Sister Hammer?"

"Father did. Mother, if named Apollonia I had been, perhaps I would have had black hair like hers."

Sister Landis looked up sharply.

"Who was talking about your hair? A wonder it is you cannot begin and tell a story straight through!"

"Oh, Andrew and Benjamin then as usual said things. Very stupid are both of them, and grieved I would be if I were their sister! What can they read? Last winter yet they are in the book of Mark only!"

Sister Landis looked anxiously at her twelve-year-old daughter. Anna Elizabeth was rather less than average height, and while no child could look slender in a blue dress which was made of such sturdy material and which was so generously full at the waistline, or graceful in shoes that were so clumsy, still she rocked back and forward from heels to toes with a certain lilt to her movements. She had taken off her white muslin cap with the ruffle that usually framed her face, and the afternoon sun shining in on her hair, primly smooth and firmly braided, turned it to a color more red than brown. She looked up at her mother suddenly with clear brown eyes.

"Very well they could a thrashing take!"

"I will have no such talk!" said her mother sternly. "Brethren we are, and no quarreling or fighting do I want to hear of!"

"We did *not* fight!" said Anna Elizabeth. Her mouth, small and sensitive, seemed curiously at variance with a chin which, despite the soft contour of childhood, spoke unmistakably of determination. Now the mouth seemed innocent; the chin, however, looked resolute enough to prove that the pacifist doctrine, even though accepted from babyhood, did not necessarily lead to softness of character. "When they said something about a witch and red hair and such nonsense, Henry said, 'A witch! Stupid ones!' And when Andrew came up to pull my braids, only look at him I did and said, 'Suffer fools gladly!' "

The spinning wheel stopped again, this time so suddenly that the thread broke in her mother's hand. Anna Elizabeth was walking carefully along the line of sunlight on the floor, putting down each foot so that just half of it was in sunshine and the other half in shadow, and she could not look up in time to interpret her mother's ejaculation. When she did lift her eyes, her mother looked very stern indeed.

"Anna Elizabeth," she began.

"Mother," said Anna Elizabeth, "that is in the Bible." Again behind the seeming innocence of clear eyes and sensitive mouth lay the firmness of a stubborn chin. "In the lesson that father read this morning it was. We are Brethren, and so I cannot quarrel with stupid boys. Yes. Then I cannot quote scripture either?"

"It did not sound so this morning when your father read," began her mother, a little feebly. "We will ask him about this."

The sound of a wagon and horses and of voices from the barn called Anna Elizabeth to run over to the door and look out through the open upper half.

"The Frantzes it is, mother. Brother Frantz must be going to the blacksmith shop too, and Sister Frantz will be coming in." She ran into the yard where her brother Henry and her father stood greeting the newcomers.

Her father smiled at her and put his hand on her shoulder, and she stood there, looking up at her father, whom she adored, and at her ten-year-old brother, who had taken her part against the "stupid boys," and at the barnyard and fields looking particularly fresh and green in the June sunshine after the heavy rain of the morning, and at the company who had just come, and she felt delightfully at home and very happy.

She listened only halfheartedly to the conversation between her father and Brother Frantz, about crops and the weather and the blacksmith shop and the iron foundry, although she liked Brother Frantz well enough. He never said much to her, but he was tall and quiet, and he seemed very much like his son Michael. And Anna Elizabeth thought Michael was very nice indeed. When Sister Frantz started for the house, she followed after.

On the way in, her sisters came from the front yard where they had been playing and said they were hungry. So she stopped to get the bread and began spreading huge slices with apple butter for them. As she worked, she heard words from the corner of the room where her mother and Sister Frantz were already busily visiting.

"Too wet it is in the garden to be out—" The rain that morning had been unusually heavy, and that was why her mother was spinning at this hour of the day.

"—and so I said, 'I'll just ride along as far as the Landises' and visit while you go on—" Everybody in the community knew that Sister Frantz was very fond of going with her husband, Anna Elizabeth thought, as she scooped up more apple butter.

"And the little girls?" It was like her mother to ask that question. Anna Elizabeth handed the slices of bread to her sisters and took another look at the cradle to see if Samuel was still sleeping.

"Michael is at home, and good he is—" There was something else about Michael and half brother. Sister Frantz was Brother Frantz's second wife; Michael's mother had died when he was only a little boy.

Suddenly Anna Elizabeth heard her name mentioned.

"Anna Elizabeth wonders why I did not name her Apollonia," her mother was saying.

Anna Elizabeth was somewhat annoyed at this unnecessary remark. She didn't mind asking her mother questions—in fact, she liked it a great deal—but that was no reason why Sister Frantz, who talked all the time, should know them. She drew nearer.

"What a queer idea, that!" exclaimed Sister Frantz. "And what a queer child you are! Reading much of the time, Michael said once. It cannot be good for you."

"It wondered me who thought up the name," Anna Elizabeth explained patiently. "I do not want to be called Apollonia. But it wondered me why Sister Lehman thought of it and mother didn't. Do you suppose she got it from Apollos in the Bible?" The last question came suddenly, as so many of Anna Elizabeth's did.

Sister Frantz looked both shocked and pained.

"No Apollos is there in the Bible, Anna Elizabeth," she said.

Anna Elizabeth looked up quickly. Her mother, seeing the gleam in her eyes and the set of her lips, hastily interposed.

"There is an Apollos, you know," she said, half apologetically. " 'I have planted, Apollos watered; but God gave the increase.' "

"Maybe the name comes from Apollyon." This was Anna Elizabeth's second suggestion, and although she was walking along the line of sunshine again, she covertly watched both her mother and the visitor as she made it.

Sister Frantz's round, good-natured face looked so bewildered that Anna Elizabeth was almost sorry for her.

"Is there then an Apollyon in the Bible?" she asked, sighing a little.

"Not in the Bible," replied Anna Elizabeth, plunging into her explanation joyfully. "He is a foul fiend, and he has scales and wings like a dragon, and feet like a bear, and a mouth like a lion. And when he talks—"

This was too much for Sister Frantz.

"Now may heaven preserve us!" she exclaimed piously. "And where could you learn such lies? It is just as I said, Mary. She reads too much. It is not good for a girl to read so much!"

"The story is in *Pilgrim's Progress*," explained Sister Landis. "Her father tells her stories from the book. She did not read this."

"And a good man is your husband—none better, I will say—but he reads too much. Always wanting a schoolteacher for the children, and even helping his girls to learn! A woman should not know so much. How then will the child ever get married?"

"Now no cause have you to worry about that," said Sister Landis, speaking with unusual dignity. She was the kindest-hearted person in the community, but there is a limit to any woman's patience.

"A man does not like a woman to know too much," declared Sister Frantz. "What man then will marry a woman that knows more than he does? Anna Elizabeth can read better than most boys right now."

"And ashamed I would be if I couldn't!" cried Anna Elizabeth.

"Many a man marries a woman who knows more than he does," Sister Landis retorted, "marries her, and lives with her for ten years, yes, twenty even, and never does he find out that she knows more than he does. Not marry! Of course she will marry!"

"But—" Sister Frantz began.

"Look, then," interrupted Sister Landis. "Spin she can, and bake, and churn, and as good with Samuel almost as I am, she is, and minds the girls. Why should she not marry? Of course she will!"

Anna Elizabeth stood listening with wide eyes. She had always known, in a quiet, comfortable sort of way, that her father was proud of her for reading and writing as she did, but she had never heard her mother praise her so. For that matter, she had never expected it, for she knew well enough that if she could, she would drop any task assigned to her to read. Her mother happened to glance at her, and reading her expression in a moment, she was suddenly embarrassed at her outspoken praise of her child to another.

"Anna Elizabeth, take Samuel and go out in the yard this minute," she said suddenly.

Anna Elizabeth knew when to reason with her mother and when to obey without remark. Now she leaned over the cradle, reached for her small brother, who was awake but not crying, and went obediently.

On the steps outside the kitchen door her two sisters were finishing their bread. They sat like two overgrown robins, Catharine with the dark hair, Joanna with the light.

"The paper came today, not?" said Anna Elizabeth.

"Yes. Hans brought it," said Catharine.

"He asked about you," added Joanna.

"Sorry I am not to have been here," said Anna Elizabeth. "We passed him on the road."

Hans was the teamster who drove all the way from Philadelphia through Germantown up the Schuylkill Valley to the iron foundry at Oley and beyond carrying materials to and from the foundry, and iron for the blacksmiths, and produce to buy or sell for the farmers like her father and the Hammers and the Lehmans and the Frantzes, as well as all the Pennsylvania German folk. Most important of all to Anna Elizabeth, he brought the *High German Pennsylvania Recorder of Events,* which Christopher Sower published each month, and which was the only new thing Anna Elizabeth ever saw to read until a new almanac came out for another year. Its newer and shorter title, *Pennsylvania Reports,* was not nearly so impressive as the one by which she had first learned to know it. Hans left most of these papers at the shop, where the farmers got them whenever they had occasion to go there, but usually he stopped at the Landis farm when he was going farther north and gave them their copy and talked with her father. Sometimes if she and Henry had gone down the road a mile and a half to the Frantzes' house on an errand, Hans would come by and talk to them as they walked along beside him. Once he had allowed Henry to hold the lines that guided his six-horse team, and Henry was still proud of those few moments. Although there were many teamsters who drove their wagons up

the Schuylkill Valley road, Hans was the only one who
came regularly up the Manatawny River north from the
foundry. So the Landis children felt quite well ac-
quainted with him, and Anna Elizabeth could not help
regretting that she had missed her usual conversation
with the jolly teamster.

"But it was fun to go with father," she added. "The
paper is in the other room?"

The two girls nodded together.

With Samuel still in her arms, Anna Elizabeth went
through the kitchen into the front room and came back
with the paper. It was a pity not to be able to hear the
rest of the conversation, she thought, for she heard her
mother ask about Sister Lehman. Sister Lehman had
very interesting ailments, and her cures were even more
interesting—not always the kind the good Christopher
Sower gave to his people. Once Anna Elizabeth had
overheard a reference to boiling seven new needles and
seven new pins in a tin can, and she had rather wanted
to try it herself to see if the water looked different after
this strange procedure. But when she mentioned the
matter to her mother, her mother only looked at her
sharply and said, "What nonsense! And why should we
do anything so foolish?" Perhaps Apollonia Lehman
would tell her sometime what Sister Frantz was telling
her mother now.

She carried Samuel out in the yard under a tree and
then stretched out beside him, placing herself so that
she could see what he was doing with the smooth,
round pieces of wood she had given him to play with.
She opened the newspaper; then, wishing to know the
keen joy of anticipation a little longer, she closed it and
rolled over on her back. Samuel, sitting precariously,
lost his balance and fell over against her. She put out a
hand, righted him somewhat, and said soothing words.
Then she relaxed luxuriously. She was sure that she
could read one article at least before supper, no matter

what her mother asked her to do. Perhaps another minister in Philadelphia had got drunk, and the good Christopher Sower had written another article telling how evil was all kind of liquor. Perhaps there had been another sale of Negroes, and he was saying how unchristian and wicked that was. That evening at supper she would wait until the right moment and then say, "Father, I see the good Christopher Sower says—"

And her father would put down his knife, and stroke his beard, and seem to look very much surprised, although there would be something like a twinkle far back in his eyes, and he would say, "What! And is Anna Elizabeth reading the newspaper again?"

Anna Elizabeth sighed happily, and Samuel's warm, round head went up and down as he rested comfortably against her. She didn't really care about what the Hammer boys had said, and she didn't mind that she was the only little girl in the community with red hair. She had gone to the shop with her father, and she had been in an exciting argument, and she had a new paper to read. Any way you looked at it, she thought, it had been a very nice day indeed.

CHAPTER II

Dark Sayings

It was late afternoon, and Anna Elizabeth and Henry were walking leisurely down the path from the house to the barn. It wasn't quite time to start calling the cows, or if that failed, to go down the lane for them.

"Let's ask questions," suggested Anna Elizabeth. "If you could have only one kind of animal on the farm, which would you take?"

"Horse," replied Henry.

"Why?"

"Well, where would one be on a farm without a horse?"

"You can't *eat* a horse. If you chose cows, you could have milk, and beef, and you could use them to pull the plow if you had to."

"Cows are stupid. If you were learning to milk, you wouldn't choose cows."

"I can milk."

"Well, you don't do it very often," interrupted Henry, muttering to himself.

"And cows aren't stupid. They come when you call them, and they remember where to go in the barn."

"What about that new cow that father bought? Not once has she come up when we called since we got her. Always I have to go clear back in the field for her."

"It may not be stupid she is; maybe she is just contrary."

"That is worse than stupid."

"It isn't." Anna Elizabeth's voice was final. "Henry, do you wish father would still have oxen?"

"No. They are too slow. They were all right when the land was being cleared, but horses are much better." Henry sounded very important as he answered his sister's question.

"I can remember the team of oxen. I was afraid of them."

"Afraid!" Henry looked surprised. "I did not know you were ever afraid."

Anna Elizabeth did not reply. She herself could not tell why she did not talk about it. Catharine had cried when the big gander had chased her, and Joanna was still afraid of the turkey gobbler, and she knew exactly how they felt. But she was older, and Henry thought she was as brave as he, and there was no use in discussing the matter.

"It is your turn to ask a question," she said.

"What kind of a tree would you rather have?" asked Henry, lying down comfortably under a huge maple.

"Fruit tree?" asked Anna Elizabeth. "If so, not cherry!" And she looked at her hands, which were stained after an afternoon of seeding cherries. Her mother was even then stirring the last ones in the large preserving kettle with molasses enough that they could be put in crocks and kept all winter.

"Any kind," insisted Henry.

"If you didn't have one kind of trees, you couldn't build houses and barns, and if you didn't have the other kind, what would you eat? That is too hard."

"No harder than choosing between horses and cows."

"Well, I'll ask another question. Who would you

rather have exhort us then at the meeting next Sunday at the Hammers'?"

Henry chewed a long grass stem for a moment and thought about this. Anna Elizabeth seated herself on a stump not far off and twisted her fingers in and out in a dozen different ways as she waited. Her hands might get tired, but they were seldom quiet.

"I think I wish that Brother Kline would come and preach," he said at last.

"Why?" It was one of Anna Elizabeth's favorite words.

"Well," said Henry, a little irritably, "a preacher ought to be able to preach better than someone else who just gets up and talks, oughtn't he?"

"That isn't saying he always does," retorted Anna Elizabeth, gesturing decisively. "I think I would wish for Brother Peter Becker to come. He does not shout when he preaches, and very nicely does he have us sing."

"It is too far for him to come."

"He is at Skippack now, and not at Germantown. That is not so far. And Brother Duboy is coming sometime this summer from Great Swamp. Mother said so. That is almost as far."

"Well, you can choose him if you want to," Henry said, in no mood to argue over this matter.

"Henry," said Anna Elizabeth suddenly, "just suppose then some of the brethren from Ephrata would come! They used to go about preaching. Maybe Peter Miller would come. Seven languages can he read!"

"Or Stephen Koch, who sees visions then! I would like to see him!"

"Or Conrad Beissel himself! I would like to have him come. And I suppose Apollonia Lehman would believe every word he said!"

"Would you?"

"No, but I would like to hear him." Anna Elizabeth

paused and sighed a little. "But father would not like to see them come."

The Ephrata people were a group under the leadership of Conrad Beissel, most of whom had originally been members of the Dunker Church, to which Anna Elizabeth's parents belonged. The Dunkers (so called by their neighbors, although they themselves usually referred to each other simply as Brethren) had settled originally at Germantown, and now were scattered in a fan-shaped area north and west in the Pennsylvania colony. After Beissel's group withdrew from the mother church, they settled at Ephrata, only about thirty miles away, and the feelings of the different Brethren toward them varied from bitter disagreement and hostility all the way to tolerance, sympathy, and almost complete belief. A visit from the Ephrata brethren was sure to stir up heated discussions, and Anna Elizabeth, however great her curiosity to see one of these men herself, knew that her father would not wish for this.

Henry rolled over and sat up again.

"Whoever then does the exhorting," he observed, preparatory to getting up, "Brother Hammer will lead in prayer. Very powerful in prayer he is."

"Very powerful," agreed Anna Elizabeth. "Do you remember then two weeks ago how Samuel cried? Not one bit did it worry him!"

"Anna Elizabeth!" It was her mother's voice from the kitchen.

"Samuel will be awake again, I suppose," she said, rising resignedly. "Rocked him I did all during that last pan of cherries, too, and my foot is still tired."

Neither of the two wishes about the meeting was fulfilled the following Sunday, for there was no minister present. The members of the Oley congregation, who lived on either side of the Manatawny River, had no resident preacher, and so often there was none to speak at their Sunday gatherings. But Anna Elizabeth's father

read the scripture and talked for a while, and Anna
Elizabeth thought to herself that her father said more
sensible and worth-while things in a short time than
some ministers did in a much longer time. Brother
Hammer prayed, and Samuel did not cry this time, and
they sang the hymn of Peter Becker's which Anna Elizabeth liked very much.

> If at present thou dost suffer
>   On the narrow way
> Scoffing, keep straight on the right path,
>   Still shun the broad way.
> Do men look at thee askance?
> Art thou grieved?   Have patience!
>
> Trust me, truly comes the time
>   This shall pass away.
> Strife, contentions, all shall leave
>   Him who still shall pray.
> Keep thy faith and valiance,
> Contend for truth.   Have Patience!

There were a great many stanzas in the hymn, and
Anna Elizabeth liked some of them better than others.
She thought it was a good hymn to sing before Brother
Hammer prayed. At first she listened to him very carefully that Sunday morning, then she fell to wondering if
he ever prayed so powerfully for his sons, who seemed
to her so impervious to learning, and then she felt
ashamed and tried to decide what her worst sin was.
Brother Hammer arrived at his *amen* before she came
to any definite conclusion, but she arose from her
kneeling position by the bench with Brother Becker's
hymn still singing in her mind and with charity in her
heart even for the Hammer boys.

In the yard Michael spoke to her. Michael was sev-
enteen years old, and so of course didn't belong in her
group of children at all. He was tall, and slow in his

movements, and often seemed both shy and awkward. But when he started to do something, he did it with a calmness and steadiness that impressed Anna Elizabeth, who was herself always quick and impulsive in her doings. Now he smiled a little as he passed her and said, "Have you read the new paper yet?"

"Of course," Anna Elizabeth said, smiling happily in return. No one outside her family ever asked her about reading except Michael.

She went on to join the group of children assembled in the yard—Lehmans, Apollonia with the black hair and her brother Julius; the Hammer boys and their little sisters; the Frantz girls, Hannah and Maria, who were only a trifle older than Catharine and Joanna; the Schreibers; the Stamms, and others.

"Let's all walk down the lane as far as the big tree," suggested one, and after much calling back and forth between children and parents, and much warning from the latter about being careful of clothes, the older ones started off. Even the Hammer boys walked along to be in the crowd.

"Your mother is better, I think, since she was at the meeting this morning," said Anna Elizabeth politely to Apollonia.

"Better, yes, but the misery in her bones is something awful," said Apollonia. "Very strange it is, and it wonders us what is the matter."

"Did your father then send for some medicine from the good Christopher Sower?" asked Anna Elizabeth.

"She has medicine, yes," replied Apollonia, looking doubtfully first at Anna Elizabeth and then at the Schreiber girls. "I do not know," she went on, keeping her eyes on Dorothea Schreiber, "whether I should tell you what she is doing or not."

"It matters not," replied Anna Elizabeth promptly, her chin held high. These other girls were almost all older than she by a year or so, but she was easily the most independent person in the group.

"So many things you do not know, Anna Elizabeth," said Dorothea apologetically.

"About witches and magic and such things?"

"Well, everybody knows that very strange things happen," declared Apollonia, shaking her black braids solemnly. "Surely you know, then, that cream is sometimes bewitched and the butter will not come."

"And then you drop a hot iron in the cream to drive out the witch," said Anna Elizabeth, smiling.

"Sure. And what else would you do?"

"And then the person in the neighborhood with the burned mark is the witch!" Anna Elizabeth's voice registered amusement touched with scorn. "Mother sets the cream near the fire before we begin to churn, not, Henry? And never have we used the hot iron!"

"Right!" said Henry.

"Next month is the time to drive away insects and bugs and such," offered Julius. "On July 15 the apostles were dispersed to preach the gospel to every creature, and so on that day you can drive away pests."

"Tschk!" It was no word Anna Elizabeth said, only an inarticulate exclamation of disgust and unbelief.

"Do you never read the Sower almanac then?" cried Benjamin Hammer.

"The good Christopher Sower does not believe such stuff, I know. Father says he does not."

"He prints the saints' days," declared Benjamin triumphantly.

"Only so that some of you will know when to plant potatoes or sow clover," cried Anna Elizabeth hotly. "It is the only way he can tell you about when the right time will be. Was he frightened by the comet three years ago? He was not!"

"The comet was more than three years ago," said Apollonia.

"It was the winter of '43 and '44. This is 1747."

"He prints the saints' days," repeated Benjamin stubbornly.

"Do you know how to make strong vinegar?" asked Andrew Hammer. "After you have put the cider in the barrel and before you set it away, blow into the bunghole hard and say the names of the seven crossest women you know, and oh, but the vinegar will make good!"

"And why not the names of men, then?" retorted Anna Elizabeth. "Or boys? Very strong vinegar could I make!"

"Anna Elizabeth, you will learn sometime not to be so unbelieving," said Apollonia gravely.

"Look who is coming down the road!" her brother Julius exclaimed.

The children stopped talking and grouped together haphazardly. At the turn of the road just below the big tree came a small, bent woman walking slowly. There was a murmur of voices. "Who then—" "Never did I see her—" "Hush! Do you suppose—"

Anna Elizabeth stood watching, wide-eyed. Although the woman walked slowly, she did not seem feeble. But her hair was gray, her face covered with wrinkles, and her clothing more tattered and dirty than anything Anna Elizabeth had ever seen. She seemed to be talking to herself as she approached, but she stopped as she saw the children. Then her gaze fell on Anna Elizabeth, and Anna Elizabeth was startled at the piercing black eyes. The woman watched the girl for some time, even after she resumed her walking, and Anna Elizabeth returned her gaze, pity and curiosity alike expressed in her straightforward brown eyes. Then the woman looked down again, and started muttering, and so passed out of hearing.

"Well!" exclaimed Apollonia. "Now what do you think?"

"Where do you suppose she is going, Henry?" asked Anna Elizabeth. "Do you think she lives with some of the workers at the foundry? But why is she alone?"

"She does not look as if she belonged to anybody," said Henry.

"How she did look at you, Anna Elizabeth," said Apollonia. Dorothea and Susan Schreiber nodded agreement.

"If again our cow gets lost," began George Stamm.

Anna Elizabeth looked at him impatiently. "When then did you fix your fences last?" she demanded.

"She could not *see* our stock coming up the road as she did," said Andrew Hammer.

"Oh," cried Anna Elizabeth. But just then one of the light wagons drove up. It was the Frantzes, and since they had brought the Widow Stamm and her children with them, George left the group now. The Landis wagon came next.

"*Something* will happen," declared Apollonia solemnly, as Henry and Anna Elizabeth climbed into the wagon.

Eagerly they told their parents about the strange woman, raising their voices above the noise of the wagon wheels and the harness.

"And really, mother, I think Apollonia and Andrew and the rest are afraid because she went by," said Anna Elizabeth.

"The poor woman!" exclaimed her mother. "No doubt she was hungry."

"Probably she was going toward the foundry," said her father. "But do you suppose she could get work, even cleaning at the big house, if she was so old and dirty?"

"So much we have to be thankful for!" And Mary Landis looked at her children and held her baby closer.

That night as she was getting the children ready for bed, she mentioned the stranger again. "It wonders me if the poor old woman has food and a place to sleep tonight," she said.

Anna Elizabeth went over to the chair where her father sat reading, the candle on the mantel above him throwing curious shadows of him on the floor.

"Father," she began, "the old woman did look at me very much. Why do you suppose she did?"

Her father put an arm around her and stroked his beard according to his custom when he was thinking.

"I suppose, Anna Elizabeth, because it had been a long time since she had seen anyone so young, and well, and happy."

Anna Elizabeth drew a long breath.

"Yes, father," she said, and went off to sleep peacefully.

CHAPTER III

Apollyon Again

Anna Elizabeth was down along the road picking wild raspberries one afternoon. Her basket was full, and the bushes that grew along the edges of the wood and by the rail fence were pretty well picked. She wiped her face and felt that her hair was curling a little around the edges where it was damp from perspiration under her muslin cap. She had half a notion to go to the house around the road and up the lane instead of across fields, as she had come.

When she saw a team and wagon coming down the road, and a little later recognized Hans, the teamster, she was sure that the road would be the more interesting.

"Hello!" cried Hans, when he saw the little figure by the road. He was riding for a change, but he got down off the left-hand horse nearest the wagon, which was the one he rode, and held out his hand for the basket. The teamsters always rode horseback, either on one of

33

the horses in their team or on an extra one at the side. The wagons were used only for freight. "Going my way?" he asked.

Anna Elizabeth nodded. "You have no paper today, I suppose?"

"Now then!" Hans exclaimed. "And that is all you think of! Only two weeks ago I brought the paper, and it is published only once a month."

"It was the May paper, and now it is the middle of June."

"The June 16 paper I do not have. Have you read the other then?"

"Of course," replied Anna Elizabeth.

Hans hung the basket of berries by the side of the wagon and spoke to the team. Anna Elizabeth looked with an admiration that never grew dull at the huge wagon and the six sleek, strong horses. Their harness jingled, and the tar bucket at the back of the wagon swung and squeaked, and Hans marched along beside the wagon, stepping briskly in spite of his generous figure.

"And what is your father doing?"

"Making hay. Michael is helping."

"And not Anna Elizabeth?"

"I carry food and water to them. But most of the time I help mother and take care of Samuel."

"Maybe you would like to ride, then," said Hans suddenly, checking the horses. "I'll stop to say a few words to your father."

Anna Elizabeth hesitated a little. It would be very exciting to ride Hans' beautiful horse, but she felt a bit doubtful and almost afraid. Every now and then a fragment of conversation she had overheard between her father and mother came to her mind.

"But Samuel, I do not think Anna Elizabeth should be so friendly to Hans. Not of our people is he, and it wonders me—"

"He will not hurt the child."

"Of course he will not *hurt* her!"

"He will not say anything to her that he should not. I know he is not of our faith. But is she then to know nobody but Brethren people?"

"Well, you know him better than I, of course—"

"It will be all right, Mary."

Now Anna Elizabeth nodded at Hans. "I will ride," she said.

So Hans swung her up into the saddle, and there she sat, holding on awkwardly and tightly, her eyes shining with excitement, her cheeks flushed.

"So you read," said Hans conversationally.

"And write too."

"What!" exclaimed Hans. "Who then teaches a girl to write?"

"Well, the teacher father got last winter taught us at our house most of the time, and he saw the copies I made from Henry's writing book, and sometimes he would help me a little. Why should he not, then? If it had not been for father, would he have had a school here?"

"He did not get rich teaching you children."

"No." Anna Elizabeth sighed. "That's why we could not have him longer—there was so little money. Only two months he taught us, and maybe he will not come back next year."

"Very unusual is your father. He has a good farm, yes, and you are not hungry, but all that money for learning—! Why, I know girls in Philadelphia who can't write."

"But there is a woman in Philadelphia who teaches school. A Quaker she is. I wish I could teach school."

"What nonsense! Only one such in Philadelphia there is, I think, and that enough, no doubt!"

"Mother can write. She learned in Germany. Why shouldn't I?"

Hans shook his head. "Very unusual is your father," he repeated.

"Yes," Anna Elizabeth agreed, "father is different." There was a little pause, and the noises of the horses and the wagon became prominent again. "We all are different."

Hans looked up at the straight little figure on the horse.

"By—that is—" Here Hans was taken with a fit of coughing. He came out of it red in the face and chuckling. "What I mean is, you're quite right! Who then will bring you your paper if I do not come up this road any more?"

Anna Elizabeth looked down in astonishment. Hans had been a fairly regular part of her life for several years now.

"But what would you do?" she asked.

"I might try the road through Conestoga, and go as far as Harris' Ferry," he said.

Anna Elizabeth's eyes grew wide with wonder.

"Almost to the mountains? Aren't there Indians out there?"

"I might turn soldier."

"But—"

"I forgot!" Hans looked sheepish. "You think that is very wrong. Well, I really don't think I'll be a soldier, but I might—well, go away from this country."

"Why?"

"Well—" This seemed to be Hans' favorite word for the moment. He kicked at clumps of grass as he walked along the narrow road. "Well, this year 1747 has not been so good for Hans. Sometimes very easy it is just to go away."

"Sometimes very hard it is to go away," said Anna Elizabeth wisely. "Christian would have run away from Apollyon only he had no armor for his back. So he had to stay and fight."

"Wh—what?" cried Hans, looking startled. "You little witch! How could you— What I mean is, where did you get such ideas?"

Anna Elizabeth looked surprised.

"Part of a story it is," she explained. "In *Pilgrim's Progress.* Christian met Apollyon in the Valley of Humiliation, and he wanted to run away, but he remembered that he had no armor for his back. So he fought Apollyon and overcame him, and a hand came to him with leaves from the tree of life, and he was healed immediately."

"*Pilgrim's Progress,*" repeated Hans thoughtfully. "I have seen that book."

"Seen it?" exclaimed Anna Elizabeth. "You mean you could read it?"

"Why, I guess I could," Hans replied.

A brilliant idea flashed into Anna Elizabeth's mind.

"Oh, Hans, won't you read it for me?" she begged, leaning toward him in her eagerness. "You could read just a little bit before you start out on the road each time and tell it to me when you stop here."

"But—"

"Hans, father read only part of the book, a long time ago, in Germantown it was. And what he read he tells me. But Christian set out for the City of Zion, and how then will I ever know how he got there? Who else did he meet on the way? And did he have other fights then? Never will I get to see the book! Published in Germany it was, and translated from the English, and how would I get it? Father never sees any more the man who had it. Won't you read it for me?"

Hans walked along moodily.

"Who ever heard of a teamster reading books?" he muttered. "And I do not think I want to read that book anyway!" This last sentence he said in a louder tone.

Anna Elizabeth bit her lip hard and said no more. She was suddenly very close to tears, and she had no intention of crying in front of Hans. But somehow she had never thought so much about this book before. She had listened eagerly to her father's stories, but now she could see the book, real, a something to be held in one's hands and read over and over again by the fire-place. Perhaps it had clasps like the Sower Bible of her father's. Perhaps it was like the *A B C Book* which she and Henry used, and out of which Catharine and Joanna and Samuel would also learn to read. And Hans had seen it, and he would not read it.

She was glad when they turned in at the barnyard. Her father and Michael were just finishing a load of hay, and her father came to lift her off the horse.

"A nice ride Hans gave you, not?" he said.

Anna Elizabeth still could not talk. She only nodded, and without so much as a glance toward Michael, she started straight for the house.

However, Anna Elizabeth knew full well that there was never time for crying. As she winked back the tears, she heard her mother call to her from the garden.

"Take the loaves of bread out of the oven, Anna Elizabeth, and see why Samuel is crying. And look where the girls are."

When she came out from the kitchen with Samuel on her arm, her mother called again. "And take Hans and the others then some milk to drink."

So she brought a pitcher of milk, and went out with it in one hand and a mug in the other, and Samuel still on her arm. Michael and her father were talking to Hans, and Hans was saying, "Well, I will see then what I can do, but it isn't mine, you know."

The men all took a drink, and Hans handed her the basket of raspberries.

"You did not mean to give them to me, did you?" he asked.

Anna Elizabeth shook her head and still did not smile.

"Tired?" asked Michael, helping her adjust the basket on the arm that held Samuel, and whistling to the baby.

Again Anna Elizabeth only shook her head, but she felt a little comforted as she went back toward the house.

That night her father said nothing at all about either her or Hans, and after the supper dishes were washed and the heavy skillets and kettles all in their places, she got out the set of Sunday-school cards which her father had brought for them from the Sower press at Germantown. Anna Elizabeth had divided the set of 381 cards into little groups of ten each, and she was memorizing each group before she read the next one.

"Do you want to guess?" she asked Henry.

"All right," he said. "Where are you now?"

"In the one hundred forties," she replied. "Ask me the Bible verses first."

"Job 22: 21, 22," Henry called.

" 'Acquaint now thyself with him, and be at peace: thereby good shall come unto thee. Receive, I pray thee, the law from his mouth, and lay up his words in thine heart.' "

"I want to play," cried Catharine.

"Me too," chimed in Joanna.

"Let them read the letters, Henry," said Anna Elizabeth. "And Catharine can say the words that she knows."

"That takes too long," objected Henry.

"Then ask me five questions, and I'll ask you five, and then I'll let the girls do five."

"1 Timothy 1:5," called Henry next.

" 'Now the end of the commandment is charity out of a pure heart, and of a good conscience, and of faith unfeigned.' "

"Too long it will take for five questions around,"

said her mother from her side of the fireplace. "Bedtime it is for the little ones."

"I'll let them do their cards first," said Anna Elizabeth. "And you can study, Henry. You are way behind me now."

"I do not mean to learn them all as you do," said Henry. "And I can read them now." But he selected another bunch of cards from the oblong leather case in which they came and began reading them.

Anna Elizabeth went to work conscientiously with her little sisters; and her father, watching her, smiled to himself. He had taught Anna Elizabeth her letters, and now no one in the family would grow up not knowing them.

When the girls went off to bed with their mother, Henry declared that he was sleepy. "Father can ask you your other three questions," he said, handing up the one hundred forties.

"And what is Luke 19:41, 42?" her father asked.

" 'And when he was come near, he beheld the city, and wept over it, saying, If thou hadst known, even thou, at least in this thy day, the things which belong unto thy peace! but now they are hid from thine eyes.' "

"And the verse?"

"It is called, *Today! Today!*

> "Each moment is a gift from God,
> So squander time then never!
> Watch, and pray, and work right well,
> Or late you will be ever."

"Very good!"

"Father," said Anna Elizabeth, interrupting him as he was ready to ask the next question, "did you hear anything of the old woman we saw that day?"

"No," he replied. He paused a little; then as his wife returned to the room, he spoke to her. "Mary, what do

you think Michael told me today? The Widow Stamm's
cow is lost."

"Not!" exclaimed his wife.

"*Do* they fix their fences?" asked Anna Elizabeth,
sitting up very straight. And then, "What will Apollonia say!"

"And now what must be done?" asked her mother.
"Food they must have, and their garden is very ordinary. But maybe the cow will turn up as it did the last
time."

"Over a week it has been gone, and they have had
no milk except what the Frantzes have sent over," replied her father. "We will have to talk at the next
meeting. No poor box do we have like the Germantown
one, but something we must do."

"Father," said Anna Elizabeth, "is there such a thing
as a witch?"

Her father laid down the bunch of cards he was
holding.

"And what puts such an idea into your head?" he
inquired, looking at her quizzically.

"I told you that Apollonia was afraid when that
woman went by," Anna Elizabeth replied. "And the
girls were talking once about a woman who went by
that way, and then when some people drove down the
road right after her, they didn't see a thing of her. And
there wasn't any house where she could have stopped
either. Could a woman just disappear like that?"

"Well, you needn't worry about this woman disap-
pearing," said her mother promptly. "We didn't drive
the direction she was walking."

"I'm *not* worrying," replied Anna Elizabeth, with
perhaps more emphasis than her feelings warranted.
"I'm just wondering."

Her father found a card from an earlier group in the
case. "Do you remember twenty-five?" he asked. "In
Proverbs 18 is the verse."

" 'The name of the Lord is a strong tower,' " recited Anna Elizabeth; " 'the righteous runneth into it, and is safe.' "

"And time it is to run to bed," said Sister Landis.

"Yes, mother." Anna Elizabeth reached for the cards, arranged them carefully according to number, put them in their box, and replaced it on a cupboard shelf. As she turned to leave the room, she looked at her father. So often he would not answer a question directly. Now he had his Bible again, and he looked very safe indeed.

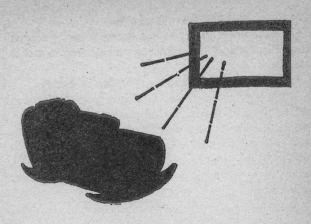

CHAPTER IV

New Kind of Seeing

It was Sunday morning again, and this time the meeting was to be at the Frantz home. Anna Elizabeth was glad, for although Sister Frantz sometimes said things that she was sure her mother thought foolish, still the two little girls and her own sisters made a nice congregation if she wanted to play church or school. They could do this if they arrived early or stayed a little late, neither of which was very probable. But it was a nice possibility just the same. And Michael never said anything much, but the boys played more quietly there than at other places, and she liked the Frantz kitchen almost as well as their own.

Now they were having morning prayers, and Anna Elizabeth was kneeling by a stool in her usual corner of the room by the table where they ate. She liked her father's prayers. It was true that she knew most of his petitions by heart, but he didn't use the same ones every day, and she usually listened quite conscientiously, particularly if something special had happened.

43

This morning the thanks and requests sounded very much as usual for a Sunday when there would be meeting. She opened her eyes and looked at the patch of bright sunlight a little to one side of her stool. At summer solstice it reached a certain crack in the floor, and she usually looked to see just where it was. Now it was the last of June, and the light had moved away from the crack ever so little. The sunlight seemed very bright that morning, and she shut her eyes tight after looking at it. There before her eyes were patches of light just the shape of the sunlight on the floor. She winked hard, but still they were there. She opened her eyes to look at the real sunlight, shut them again, and again she saw the dancing spots of light.

"For thine is the kingdom, and the power—"

Anna Elizabeth came to with a start and got to her feet just at the right moment.

That morning as they drove to Brother Frantz's home, she tried looking at the sun. It was so bright that she looked away again very quickly indeed, and when she shut her eyes, the round bright spots kept sailing away and away, and then when she winked, they came close and danced away again.

"Father," said Henry, "do you think that new cow will ever learn to come up in the evening with the others? Always she stays way back in the far grove of trees, and I have to go clear over there for her."

"Too bad it is that Rover died," said Sister Landis.

"So it is," agreed Anna Elizabeth fervently. She had liked their dog quite as much as Henry did.

"I might have found another dog this spring," Brother Landis reminded them, "but the children wanted to wait."

"We will wait for the next puppies at the Frantzes'," Anna Elizabeth said firmly. "First choice do we get, Michael says."

"But it is very long," agreed Henry. "There will be

no dog to help with the cows any more this summer. Will the new cow never learn, father?"

"I do not know," said Brother Landis. "Perhaps if you milk one cow every night this summer, Anna Elizabeth could bring the cows in by herself."

"The cow!" exclaimed Henry. "Almost always the others come in when I call."

"I could," said Anna Elizabeth, shutting her eyes once again. The sun spots were still there.

Brother Kline was at church this morning, and so there was a sermon. Quite a few people were present, and since it was very hot, benches and stools and chairs were carried out and the meeting was held outside. The women, for the most part strong and capable, were in their best dresses of blue or brown or green, the material being homespun and home-dyed. Their white caps and aprons helped to soften their faces and the rather bright colors of their dresses. The sturdy, dark suits of the men were more sober in appearance. Anna Elizabeth and some of the children sat on blankets spread out on the ground. The girls were miniature replicas of their mothers, in the same plain dresses, the same white caps and aprons. When Anna Elizabeth had looked very hard at Brother Kline, and listened very carefully, she looked away, and she could see the outline of his head and shoulders against the bright sky. She could see it very plainly with her eyes shut too.

After the meeting there was food, also served out in the yard: bread and butter, great platters of meat, cheese, pies, and fruit. The Stamms were all there, but Anna Elizabeth could see her father talking to Brother Kline, and then each of them talking to others, and she knew that the news about the lost cow was going around and that they were talking about what to do. It was so hot that even the children had no desire to do anything very strenuous. They sat around in groups and argued, for the most part good-naturedly.

"Making a sampler, I am," said Apollonia. "And mother says I may have it and put it away for my chest when I get married."

Anna Elizabeth looked a little startled. Was Apollonia that much older than she?

"Have you started a chest then, Anna Elizabeth?"

"No," replied Anna Elizabeth briefly.

"You should," said Apollonia. "Twelve you are."

"I have made many things," said Anna Elizabeth, "but no chest do I have."

"Mother says my quilting is very good," remarked Dorothea. "All by myself I am doing a quilt, a little every day. How is your quilting now, Anna Elizabeth?"

"Just medium," Anna Elizabeth said. She leaned back against a tree and watched the white summer clouds. Why should one spend a Sunday then talking only of work, she thought. She wondered if Hans were in Germantown, and if he might have relented and even now be reading in *Pilgrim's Progress*. One could read very much on a Sunday afternoon. But she was quite sure he was not reading.

"And what then do you do?" asked Apollonia impatiently.

Anna Elizabeth looked resigned.

"And what do you think then?" she inquired. "Wash dishes, and seed cherries, and pick up the new potatoes, and help with the baking, and churn, and spin a little now and then, and pull weeds in the garden, and take care of Samuel, and—"

"For yourself, I mean. What special thing are you doing? Of course everybody does what you say!"

"I am knitting mittens for Catharine and Joanna for next winter then. Will that do?" Anna Elizabeth thought of how she read a little every day, and practiced her writing sometimes if it wasn't too late when the evening work was done, but she was not in the mood for the kind of comments that were sure to follow if she mentioned this. Then she suddenly remembered her discovery of the morning. "I can see with my eyes shut," she volunteered.

Unfortunately, Andrew Hammer was circling by when she made this statement, and he raised a boisterous and jeering shout.

"Sees with her eyes shut!" he yelled. "Sees with her eyes shut!"

"What do you mean?" "Now no one can see—" "What nonsense!" The girls sat up in curiosity and amazement, and the boys came running to see what had happened.

"Anna Elizabeth can see with her eyes shut!" chanted Andrew, still in loud derision. "Shut your eyes then and catch me!"

"You laugh when I say that the old woman went past, and just three days afterward the Widow Stamm's cow was lost, and then you talk like this!" Apollonia sounded very smug and virtuous.

Anna Elizabeth's original intention had been to explain what she had discovered that morning and to let the girls experiment for themselves. Now, naturally enough, she was only very angry and in no mood for any explanations or modifications whatever.

"I can see with my eyes shut!" she declared, springing to her feet to face the noisy children. "I can." She stood with arms defiantly akimbo. "Just because you cannot do a thing, you think it cannot be done!"

"Sees with her eyes shut!" cried Andrew.

"And what is all this?" asked Michael, walking up and speaking slowly. "Did you boys see the colt yet? Just came up the lane to the barn, he did, with his mother."

The boys started racing off toward the barn, and the girls followed sedately, as became their Sunday dresses. Anna Elizabeth, still very stiff and defiant and angry, was left alone with Michael.

"Well?" Michael said, smiling his slow smile.

Anna Elizabeth looked down and felt a little foolish.

"Michael, I *can* see with my eyes shut," she said, looking up at him again. Michael's eyes were very blue, and as calm and quiet as hers were now dark and stormy.

"But better it is to keep them open, not?" suggested Michael. It was half a question, half a statement.

"But I *can* see," she insisted, no longer angry, just very much in earnest.

"Only things you have seen before," replied Michael thoughtfully.

Anna Elizabeth smiled in surprise and delight. "But of course!" she agreed.

"And so it is better to keep them open most of the time," Michael repeated. "Have you seen these, then?" And they walked toward the corner of the rail fence where a small bush of wild roses was in bloom.

Anna Elizabeth looked at the flowers, delicate and graceful in their growing, and she felt ashamed. She hadn't noticed them before. Perhaps she did keep her eyes shut too much, and read too much, and dream too much. Michael saw things that she didn't.

"Worth seeing, yes?" said Michael, watching the face on which every passing emotion was mirrored with startling vividness.

"Yes, Michael," she said meekly.

"Going to Germantown I am this winter," he told her, as they walked on toward the children and the colt.

"Why?" she asked in surprise.

"To stay with my uncle and learn weaving."

Anna Elizabeth realized anew how much older than she and the other children Michael was. Then she remembered *Pilgrim's Progress*. The book her father had read he had seen in Germantown.

"Michael, if you should see the book *Pilgrim's Prog-*

ress, wouldn't you read it for me and tell me about it next summer?"

"If I could," he agreed. "And you will keep the eyes open most of the time?"

"Yes, Michael."

Later that evening in the family circle around the fireplace where the candles always were placed even though the fire was covered, Anna Elizabeth asked a question.

"What then will you do about the lost cow?"

"We will have a business meeting after the next church service and maybe get enough money promised to buy a new one before winter."

"Michael is going to Germantown to learn weaving," Anna Elizabeth announced.

"Is he?" asked her mother.

"Yes, he told me when he was helping with the hay," her father said. "And a good thing it is for the boy."

"Sophia Frantz thinks now he will probably marry Apollonia," said Sister Landis.

"Humph!" sniffed Anna Elizabeth. "And several months ago she sat in our kitchen and was grieving because no interest in the girls he took at all, and suppose he never got married!"

"Anna Elizabeth!" said her mother reprovingly, looking across the hearth at her husband, who was reading and smiling.

"He will go to the Sunday afternoon meetings at Germantown and marry some girl from there then if he is wise," Anna Elizabeth declared.

"Father," said Henry, "back to the field again I went tonight for that cow!"

His father laid aside his book.

"Anna Elizabeth, what would you rather have if you could have your choice for a present then?"

"A book," she replied instantly. "A book for my very own."

"Well, one can never be entirely sure, but wheat looks very good, and corn also, and food we will have for the winter easily and some money besides. Suppose you take this stubborn cow for your special care for the rest of the summer, and Henry will milk his cow every night, and this fall when I go to Germantown maybe we can have some presents. Very good you have been to teach the girls their letters."

Anna Elizabeth was quite overwhelmed.

"A book for Henry too?" she asked.

"Henry and I will talk, eh, son? Very clever fingers he has, and with some tools, he might grow up to be a good carpenter then."

Henry smiled at his father joyfully. Anna Elizabeth sighed deeply in pure delight.

"A book!" she said. "Will you go to the October fair in Germantown then?"

"Well, one doesn't need to go to the fair to get a book," her father replied, smiling. "I usually go in August, and then again before winter."

"August! But that isn't long to wait at all!"

"You are not afraid to get the cows?" her father asked.

"Oh, no," she replied recklessly. Then, because she was very honest, and because she often was very much afraid of many things, like the dark, and thunderstorms, she qualified her statement a little. "Not ever enough to hurt!"

"Very well, then, we'll see," said her father, looking as happy as his children.

Anna Elizabeth sat looking into the fireplace, where scarcely a live coal could be seen under the covering of ashes. Sunday evenings were particularly nice, for no one worked at all then. Her father could read all evening, and even her mother's fingers were quiet. Now she shut her eyes tight. It was as easy as could be to see the flames shooting up the chimney as they did in the

winter time, or the quieter fire over which her mother
had cooked supper. It wasn't exactly like seeing the
patches of sunlight after shutting her eyes as she had
done that morning, but it was very vivid. Was it really
seeing or just remembering? You could remember
things without seeing them as she was seeing the fire
now.

She could even see the schoolmaster from last
winter, and how surprised he had looked one evening
when she had asked him why you couldn't begin your
Bible lessons in Revelation once instead of always in
Genesis or Matthew. She could see her family around
the fireplace: her father reading, her brother Henry on
the floor eating an apple and kicking his heels reflectively in the air, her sisters on either side of their mother listening to one of their favorite stories of the days
when their mother had gone to school in far-off
Germany, the cradle where her baby brother lay, an energetic, broad little hand swinging now and then into
sight above the smooth red sides. How very nice it was
that you could see things that way (if it was seeing)
without actually looking at them!

She could almost see the new book which her father
would bring her, and herself sitting by the fireplace
next winter reading something new out of a book once,
not something that she had read over and over. But not
quite. Michael was probably right. You could see with
your eyes shut only what you had seen before. And
then she opened her eyes wide just to be sure that her
family were all around her as she had pictured them.
They were, and when her mother sent the children off
to bed, she went happily enough to dream of books.

CHAPTER V

"I Object"

Anna Elizabeth sat on a stool out in the yard peeling early apples. Her sister Catharine helped her at odd intervals, but most of the time she was with Joanna, who was doing some fancy building with clothespins in the yard nearby. In the house Anna Elizabeth could hear her mother singing as she was preparing the week's baking—pies, bread, and cakes to go into the oven once the fire had died down and the coals had been raked out. This afternoon the Frantzes were coming over, and Sister Frantz and her mother would peel apples in dead earnest, while Brother Frantz and Michael would help her father, this time in the wheat field. It ought to be a nice afternoon, Anna Elizabeth thought, even if she had to peel almost all the time. She could take a cold snack to the men, she was sure, and if there weren't too many apples, she could perhaps play church with the little girls.

She sat thoughtfully peeling and keeping an eye on her sisters. Catharine got up from the log cabin that she was building out of the clothespins and started across the yard.

"I want a drink," she said.

"Bring me some too," called Anna Elizabeth.

"Me too." That was Joanna's favorite phrase.

Catharine stopped at the house for a large mug and went on towards the springhouse. It was only a little way from the kitchen door, and watching her sister, Anna Elizabeth thought how silly it was ever to be afraid to make that tiny journey. But when the days were short, or supper was late, and she was finishing up the dishes after dark, Anna Elizabeth knew well enough that she did not relish the trip. Only the last evening she had gone after a pail of water, and while she had walked with even pace to the springhouse and with equally even pace back, never once looking behind her, still she knew how relieved she had been to get into the house again and within the range of the candle and firelight. She was sure that Henry was not afraid in the dark, and she saw no reason why she should be. Of course her father and mother weren't afraid. She sighed and reached for another apple.

Henry came up just then with another basket full of apples. He shared in the mug of spring water which Catharine brought and which went from one child to another, and then he stretched out on the ground for a little rest.

"Do you suppose we will have any time then to play this afternoon?" asked Anna Elizabeth.

Henry reached up for a piece of peeled apple.

"Not much," he replied, putting the quarter in his mouth at once.

"You could be the preacher, Henry."

"I do not want to be the preacher," said Henry, holding up his hand again.

Anna Elizabeth handed him the knife that Catharine

had used on her two or three apples that morning. "Make yourself right at home then!" she said crisply.

Henry put the knife back in the pan. "Eat them I will without peeling," he said.

"Would you be Brother Hammer then?"

"I do not want to pray that long," objected Henry. "Run out of things to ask for, I would."

"Easy it is," said Anna Elizabeth, a little impatiently. "You just say the same things over and over in different words."

"Why do that?" asked Henry lazily.

"Well, then who will you be?" asked Anna Elizabeth. "Do you think maybe we could let Hannah Frantz do the praying? I want to be Peter Becker and set the tune."

"You can be Peter Becker and preach and sing both," said Henry cheerfully. "Or Michael could preach."

"Michael is too old to play. You know that!" Anna Elizabeth paused a moment and then added regretfully, "And a pity it is too."

"We could have business meeting," suggested Henry, "and then you could preside, and the rest of us could talk just whenever we wanted to."

"Somebody would still have to be Brother Hammer," insisted Anna Elizabeth. "He always objects!"

"So he does," agreed Henry. "Of course, a great deal of objecting all the men do in such a meeting."

"Talking they do, and a good deal of it sounds very —well, very *earnest*," said Anna Elizabeth reflectively. "It is a chair I wish I could have at the next meeting, but I know I will get a bench or else the ground. At our house is the meeting."

"Do you think other churches have such meetings?" asked Henry suddenly.

"I suppose their ministers tell the people what to do

in the big churches in Philadelphia," replied Anna Elizabeth. "We are Brethren and decide for ourselves."

"And a long time it takes," observed Henry.

"Well, Henry, you can be Brother Schreiber then," said Anna Elizabeth. "Goes to sleep he does every time the meeting lasts very long."

"How then does he know who preaches well?" Henry sat up and took a third apple. "He said last meeting that the sermon of Brother Kline in May was the most powerful he had ever heard."

"Maybe his wife tells him on the way home," said Anna Elizabeth grinning. Then she laughed outright. "Imagine mother telling father how the sermon was! Or father telling mother!"

"Now then, and what are you children talking about?" asked their mother, coming out for some of the peeled apples. "Not much work do you do when you talk so much, Anna Elizabeth!"

"Mother, do you think Sister Schreiber tells Brother Schreiber whether the sermons are good or not? You know he sleeps."

"And why do they not vote quicker instead of talking so much at the business meeting?"

"Children!" their mother exclaimed. "I want to hear no more foolish questions. Henry, hoeing there is to be done in the garden if all the apples are up now, and Anna Elizabeth will peel more apples after you have gone then. Girls, not any clothespins lost do I want. Too long it takes to whittle them. Perhaps you should use corn cobs to play with."

"I'm watching them, mother," said Anna Elizabeth.

"You know, Henry," she went on, as her mother returned to the kitchen, "father rather encourages Brother Hammer when he objects, too. Now why, do you think?"

"I do not know," said Henry, and he started for the garden, where a hoe hung conveniently by the gate.

The Frantzes arrived after an early dinner, and Sister Frantz and Anna Elizabeth and her mother "snitzed" apples with speed and energy out in the yard, while the four little girls played within observation. Even Samuel's cradle was moved out for the time being. Anna Elizabeth listened to the conversation for a while with interest.

"It makes rain tomorrow, I think," said Sister Frantz presently.

"Perhaps," replied her neighbor. "Glad I am that the harvest is being finished today for both of us. Wheat is good."

"Very good. And did you know poor Sister Lehman is not so well again?"

"No."

"It wonders me about all the cures she uses. Three different kinds of medicines she has tried now in these three weeks."

"And what kind would it be?"

"Well, you know how Sarah Lehman is, Mary. It is in my opinion—"

"Empty the pans, then, Anna Elizabeth!"

Anna Elizabeth emptied the pans, saying nothing but thinking a great deal. Her mother was very clever. If she had not been sent away just at that moment, she might have learned more about the seven new needles and the seven new pins, or she might have heard of another remedy even more interesting.

"Very good are the two Schreiber girls," Sister Frantz was saying as Anna Elizabeth came back from the kitchen with the empty pans. "Their quilting you should see. And how do you get on, Anna Elizabeth?"

"Medium," she replied. It was in her mind to inquire if Sister Frantz thought now that Michael would marry Dorothea, but she decided that she had better not ask.

"And how is Brother Schreiber?" she inquired instead.

Sister Frantz looked astonished. Anna Elizabeth's mother surveyed her intently, just as if she could read exactly what was in her daughter's mind. What Anna Elizabeth meant, of course, was, "And is he sleepy now?" Feeling her mother's gaze, she kept her eyes on the apples and peeled away demurely.

"Well he is, but excited in his mind," said Sister Frantz. "I did not know you had heard. When last he was to the blacksmith shop, he heard a new minister exhorting, and very powerful he must have been."

Anna Elizabeth looked surprised. She could not imagine Brother Schreiber excited.

"We did not hear," said Sister Landis. "What minister would that be, then?"

"One of the New-Born," said Sister Frantz. "Have you heard then what they preach? Sister Schreiber is much concerned also."

"What do they believe?" asked Anna Elizabeth with interest.

"When they are saved, they are always saved," said Sister Frantz. "Never do they sin again. Sister Schreiber was telling me, and there is a religion, she says, that is really worth something."

"Humph," said Anna Elizabeth, chiefly to herself. Her father would not believe that, she knew.

"Visions they see, and thus they know for a surety that what they believe is true."

"Visions!" This was from Sister Landis.

Anna Elizabeth smiled a little. She herself could not have said the word with a more healthy skepticism, and she was very much pleased with her mother.

"Mary," said Sister Frantz, "people in our church have had visions. And why should you speak so?"

"Stephen Koch," said Anna Elizabeth promptly. "And in Ephrata he is!"

"And what do you know about his visions?" asked Sister Frantz sharply.

"Nothing," replied Anna Elizabeth. "Have you read them then?"

"No time do I have to read," said Sister Frantz virtuously. "But that men should see things when their eyes are shut in sleep is not a thing to be laughed at. Men had visions in the Bible, not?"

"When their eyes are shut!" The phrase stayed in Anna Elizabeth's mind, and she thought of the Sunday when she had insisted that she could see when her eyes were shut. She felt a little unsettled in her mind, although she was still sure that she would not like the New-Born preacher.

"And good people are in Ephrata right now," went on Sister Frantz severely.

"Who?" asked Anna Elizabeth.

Sister Frantz had that slightly pained look on her face again. So often did she not feel exactly at ease with Anna Elizabeth.

"Maria Christina Sower is there," she said, plucking up her courage, "and she is the wife of the good Christopher Sower you are always talking about."

"I will say this, then," said Sister Landis, laying down her knife. "If good it is to leave your husband and child and go off and live in a cloister for ten years, and more, then she is very good, that is true. But if Conrad Beissel were to come here, it is then—"

Anna Elizabeth was listening to her mother with delight. There were times when she felt that she was quite as much like her mother as like her father. But when her mother looked at Anna Elizabeth, she paused.

"I did not say," began Sister Frantz feebly.

Anna Elizabeth's mother stood up very straight and picked up one of the pans.

"Much that passes for religion is very great nonsense," she said firmly. "When I know how this New-Born minister lives, I will perhaps listen to his visions, not before! Anna Elizabeth, take then something to eat to your father and the others."

Anna Elizabeth went into the house to get the food ready. Later she started toward the field with a basket over her arm and a pitcher in her hand. Henry came out of the garden to accompany her and share in the afternoon food. They walked along for a while in silence.

"It does not look like playing anything today," Henry said at last.

"No," agreed Anna Elizabeth.

"And an easy job you have," he declared, wiping his face with his handkerchief.

Anna Elizabeth ignored this slighting remark.

"Henry, Sister Frantz says that the Schreibers are listening to a new preacher who sees visions and says one can be converted and then never sin. Do you think men can see visions?"

"Stephen Koch sees them, doesn't he?"

Anna Elizabeth walked along thoughtfully.

"Do you know that if you look at something very bright, like the sunlight on the floor, or the sun, or something like that, and then shut your eyes, you can see it still?"

"Can you?" Henry looked at his sister with interest and respect. He had not shared in the altercation at the Frantz home that Sunday afternoon. "I'll try it. But I can't see that it does you any good," he added after a moment.

Anna Elizabeth smiled at this practical remark.

"Maybe Stephen Koch's visions don't do anybody any good either," she suggested.

Henry sighed profoundly. "It's hot," he said, returning to his original idea, "too hot for hoeing."

"Tired then?" asked Michael, coming to meet them in time to hear this remark. His father and Brother Landis were with him.

Henry nodded vigorously and went on mopping with one hand while he reached for food with the other.

"And you?" Michael said to Anna Elizabeth.

She looked at her hands, brown from the apples. "Rather," she said.

The men ate their bread and cold sliced meat hastily, and the mug went round and round.

"Father," said Anna Elizabeth, "why does Brother Hammer object so much in the business meetings?"

Brother Frantz looked rather startled at this frank question.

"Anna Elizabeth," replied her father, regarding her solemnly, "you can ask harder questions than anybody else I know."

"Why do you keep saying, 'And if there are no more objections'? Only encourages him it does to think up more."

Her father looked as if he might be almost ready to smile, but he didn't.

"Working time it is," he said, and he took another drink and started away. Brother Frantz followed.

"He could have answered that last question, couldn't he?" Anna Elizabeth said to Michael.

"Well," said Michael slowly.

"Do you know the answer, Michael?" she asked.

"Well," Michael said again, more slowly than ever.

Anna Elizabeth sighed. "And why then will you not tell me?"

"Better it is to find out some things for one's self," Michael said, smiling down into the eager brown eyes. And he, too, turned to the work again.

"Do you think he knows?" asked Henry.

"Oh, yes."

"Do you think you can find out?"

Anna Elizabeth gathered up the things to be taken back to the house. Her slender, capable fingers moved easily but mechanically. She was not thinking of dishes and food, but rather of the startled look on Brother Frantz's face (perhaps Michael did not ask his father questions as she did hers) and of the half-solemn, half-amused expression on her father's face and of Brother Hammer's bulky figure when he shifted himself from one position to another in a chair and puffed out his cheeks and said, "Brethren, I object!" How different men were!

"Do you?" repeated Henry.

"Yes," said Anna Elizabeth. And as she started back toward the house, she continued to think—of the New-Born minister and of Stephen Koch and of visions generally—and she reflected that she had a good many things to find out.

CHAPTER VI

Discovery

The morning of the day for church and the business meeting dawned clear but very hot. Anna Elizabeth felt sleepy even at the breakfast table. Samuel had cried in the night, and she had heard him. Her mother had sung to him and soon quieted him, and that in itself was all right. Anna Elizabeth loved the sound of her mother's singing at night, for once Samuel was quiet, she felt safe and quiet and protected. Even the darkness became peaceful and comforting when her mother sang.

But once awake, she had not been able to go to sleep again for a while. All the things she had wondered about in the last weeks came back to be thought over again. Could it be true that some women had the power of the evil eye? She was reasonably sure that her father did not believe so. Why had anyone ever started such stupid stories about people with red hair? It might be true that a bad temper was an accompaniment (Anna Elizabeth knew well enough that she had *that*), but the Hammer boys' ideas that if one had red hair, she might work some sort of magic—well, that was silly. Why should the color of one's hair have anything to do with what went on in her mind? Hans had called her a little witch. What had he meant by that? Hans was late, because there had been no July newspaper yet. Maybe he would not come at all, as he had said.

Anna Elizabeth rolled over in bed. Why did people get excited over somebody like the New-Born minister, she wondered. The Schreibers did not get excited over their own preachers. What would Brother Hammer have thought if he could have heard it? And would he object as much as usual that afternoon in the business meeting? Very hot it was going to be for much protesting. How much money would it take for a new cow for the Widow Stamm? And how many books could one buy with that much money? George Stamm had not much character; Anna Elizabeth felt sure that if it had been Michael living with his mother and a lot of little children, no cow would have been lost. Nor would it have happened if Henry had been there.

Joanna roused at this moment and called for a drink. Her mother came in softly with the water, and Catharine turned over and also asked for a drink. Anna Elizabeth moved restlessly again and opened her eyes.

"And are you awake too?" asked her mother. "Now go back to sleep, all of you." She straightened pillows and the light bed covers and went quietly back to the other room.

Now that her eyes were open, Anna Elizabeth could see the window and the curtain that separated a corner of the room where Henry slept. She lifted her head just a little, but she could see nothing through the oiled paper at the window. She was glad that they had glass downstairs. The moon must be shining very brightly, she thought, and she wished that she could see it. She fell to thinking about the moon, then, and how far away it was. Suppose you traveled and traveled and traveled until you finally could touch it and see what the marks on its face really were, even then there would be more space. The moon wasn't pasted against

the sky; when you got to it, you could go and go and
go, and maybe finally reach a star. And even then that
was no stopping place, for you could go on and on and
on. Anna Elizabeth grew tired simply thinking of it,
and she put out her hands and touched the sides of her
bed, glad for something tangible and measurable after
her journey through space.

She shut her eyes again, and pictures danced before
them of people and scenes she loved: the fireplace, and
her family around it as they had been that Sunday evening when she had closed her eyes and tried to see
things so; the harvest moon, large and red above a
cornfield when the corn was in shocks and the pumpkins lay yellow and shining in between; the sun going
down in the west behind the woods and the yellow evening star coming out, on which you could make a wish;
her baby brother, who reached out his hands to her
now most beguilingly and held her tightly around the
neck when she suggested putting him down again.
Would she have visions then when she grew older? And
if so, would she tell them, and would people get excited
about them? Or would they think, "Oh, well, people
with red hair are always queer"? If people with red hair
could work magic, like a witch, then how could anyone
work magic on them? And why then did the girls look
so solemn when the poor old woman watched her?
Could she find out tomorrow why her father was so
considerate of Brother Hammer when he objected?
And would Michael tell her if she got the right answer?
Eventually she fell asleep.

Washing the breakfast dishes helped to wake her up,
and since the Brethren would be eating at their place
that day, she was kept busy helping her mother get
things ready. When the people finally arrived and were
seated out in the yard, it was Brother Kline again who
preached. He read Revelation 4 for his scripture, and
then went on into the next chapter for his text and

preached on the seven seals. Anna Elizabeth didn't
think so much of the sermon; she had, as so often she
did, a distinct feeling that her father would not preach
that kind of a sermon. But phrases from the chapter
that Brother Kline had read kept going round and
round in her mind. "And, behold, a door was opened in
heaven." "And there was a rainbow round about the
throne, in sight like unto an emerald." She didn't know
why a rainbow should be "in sight like unto an
emerald," but then she wasn't exactly sure what an
emerald looked like, and the phrase was lovely anyway: "in sight like unto an emerald"; "and there was a
rainbow round about the throne, in sight like unto an
emerald." Then she went back to the first sentence.
"And, behold, a door was opened." That was lovely
too. Perhaps when you got to heaven you couldn't see
everything at once, and so there were always doors
opening forever and ever, or at least for a very, very
long time.

But after the sermon was over and the people had all
filed through the kitchen and past the narrow table
where the food was placed, and after the food was
eaten and people had sat around and talked a while
and the second meeting began, Anna Elizabeth found
herself getting very sleepy. They didn't even begin with
the Widow Stamm's difficulties. There was the fall love
feast to arrange for, and there was some talk about
ministers which Anna Elizabeth did not follow very
closely, although she knew that Brother Kline did not
come to Oley too regularly and that he already had
thoughts of going to Tulpehocken Valley. According
to her prediction of a few days ago, she was seated on
the ground, and her back got tired no matter how she
sat. She could feel her hair getting damp around the
edges under her cap, as it always did on hot Sundays,
and in spite of all her care, her white apron would get
wrinkles when she shifted from one position to another.

She wished that Henry were sitting next to her so that he could help keep her awake. But it was Apollonia instead who was beside her, and she did not intend to go to sleep with Apollonia looking on. Michael sat far away on the opposite side of the group, and he looked very solemn and grown up from his position among the men. There was no one in the church Michael's age, and Anna Elizabeth wondered suddenly if he ever was lonely. Perhaps her father had been thinking about that when he had said it would be a good thing for him to go to Germantown. One of these days he would be baptized, and then he could vote like all the other men. Maybe he would be baptized at Germantown.

In spite of all her good intentions, Anna Elizabeth found that the heads of the people began swimming round and round.

"And so far as the Widow Stamm is concerned," she heard her father saying, "Brethren we are, and we cannot let her and her children go hungry."

So they had got to that matter at last! How fortunate that the Stamms had not come to this meeting, Anna Elizabeth thought. If only she were sitting next to her mother, and could lay her head over against a stool or bench!

The heads went round and round again, and in the hot stillness of the afternoon Anna Elizabeth could hear the bees down in the orchard.

"Brethren, right it is that we should consider carefully of this trouble of the Widow Stamm. But there are a few thoughts that occur to me."

Anna Elizabeth sighed. It was Brother Hammer, of course, and she tried to concentrate on "the thoughts."

"Two or three shillings I might give—"

It would take more than two or three shillings to buy a cow, Anna Elizabeth thought angrily. And Brother Hammer owned as many acres as any of the men in their congregation.

"This is what I would suggest," said Brother Frantz's quiet voice, and Anna Elizabeth thought that so would Michael talk in meeting one of these days, not like Brother Hammer at all.

The heads spun round again and got all mixed up in a blur that went finally into blackness. Anna Elizabeth roused sheepishly a few minutes later and wondered if her mother had noticed her. Henry and Julius and the Hammer boys were seated around the trunk of a tree, comfortably dozing.

"Six shillings will I give if each one will—"

Brother Hammer again. Anna Elizabeth fought the overwhelming darkness once more.

"True it is that we might send things over, and all of us would be glad to do that, I'm sure," said Anna Elizabeth's father. "But when winter comes on—"

Her father was so wise, thought Anna Elizabeth sleepily. It was his voice that she heard next.

"And if there are no more objections," he was saying. "I suggest, Brother Kline, that we take the vote."

She waited for Brother Hammer's voice. Now he was speaking again. Would he make it eight shillings this time? And then Anna Elizabeth suddenly sat up very straight, wide awake. Every time he had talked, he had increased the number of shillings. So *that* was why her father always saw to it that he could talk as much as he wanted to! The more he talked, the more he gave.

The vote was favorable, and they were making subscriptions now.

"Eight shillings." That was from Brother Schreiber, and it was all right. They did not own much land.

"Ten shillings," said Brother Frantz, and Anna Elizabeth smiled a little.

"Six shillings." This was from the Kempfers, who lived across the Manatawny and whom Anna Elizabeth did not know so well.

"Twelve shillings." It was the price of a book, Anna

Elizabeth thought, but she was very proud of her father just the same.

"Ten shillings." It was Brother Hammer who spoke so distinctly.

Across the intervening space, Anna Elizabeth's eyes looked straight at Michael's. He was looking just as straight at her, not smiling, not moving at all. But his quiet blue eyes were smiling, and they said just as plainly as could be, "You see?"

"I do," said Anna Elizabeth's brown ones in return, and her lips began to smile too. But she remembered that she was in church (even if the meeting was being held outside), and so she looked down and smoothed her apron demurely, and thought how very exciting it was to be alive and always finding out things.

That evening Anna Elizabeth's mother dished out great platters of potato soup and passed around the johnny cake and apple butter. She smiled at her husband past the children sitting on benches on either side of the table.

"And so everything was all right, father," she said.

"So," said her husband in return.

"A very good meeting it was," agreed Anna Elizabeth, with a new quality in her voice.

Her father and mother looked at each other across the table, and Henry put down his spoon.

"Why do you say that?" he demanded. "And what happened then that was so special?"

It was an important moment. Anna Elizabeth could feel her father and mother waiting to see what she would say. She loved her brother Henry, she valued his good opinion of her highly, and she was intensely loyal to him. But she felt now how right Michael was. Some things you did not tell; you just waited for people to find them out for themselves. So she spoke very casually indeed in reply.

"I just said it was a good meeting. Only I got very

sleepy. Henry, where do you suppose that cow was tonight?"

"Some place where she shouldn't be," he replied
promptly.

"Way back hidden in the trees, she was, and I believe she was trying to get over the fence. One day she
will not be in the fields even."

Again her father and mother looked at each other
over the table. Anna Elizabeth was not quite sure what
they were saying to each other, but she knew they were
saying something. Very nice it was to be able to talk
with the eyes only, and not with words, she thought,
and some day she would understand every single thing
that grown people said to each other that way.

Now she was suddenly very sleepy again. She ate
quietly, thinking that she would not try to memorize any
Sunday-school cards tonight at all. She wouldn't even
try reading a chapter from a hard book in the Bible,
like Romans or Revelation. She would read a Psalm
only, and then go straight to bed. And she was quite
sure that she would not stay awake that night, even to
think.

CHAPTER VII

Dangers Not in Evidence

It was a stormy-looking evening in late July when Anna Elizabeth started back through the field for the recalcitrant cow that had been her charge now for about a month. Clouds were gathering in the west, and there was a quietness and sultriness in the atmosphere that was a fairly certain indication of an approaching thunderstorm. There would be the first flashes of lightning before she got back to the barn, Anna Elizabeth thought, gritting her teeth a little at the prospect. She didn't see why she should be afraid of things, but she was, and since she was afraid of them, she didn't see why she should not say so. Some girls hid under the featherbeds while it lightened and thundered; she kept her eyes wide open.

The other cows had come up early, and Anna Elizabeth could not help thinking that the fourth one in their herd might have followed her example tonight. "So—oo—oo!" she called again and again, but there was no sound or motion in response to her cries. She would have to name this cow, she thought; maybe a cow would respond to a more personal appeal. Still Anna Elizabeth walked on steadily. She had set her pace when she started back to the field, and now she held to it resolutely. If she started to run, she knew well enough that she would only be more afraid. She crossed the little brook in the field by walking the log, although she could easily have jumped it if she had stayed by the fence.

When at last she arrived at the clump of trees in the far end of the pasture, the cow in question came out and stood looking at her.

"Get along now," said Anna Elizabeth sternly, clapping her hands and taking another step toward her.

The cow only gave a toss of the head, a playful leap into the air, and again stood looking at Anna Elizabeth. For the moment, Anna Elizabeth was too surprised even to be afraid. She stood still, staring. The cow tried another graceful leap, cavorted again, and this time unmistakably came toward her.

And then in truth Anna Elizabeth was terrified. She had nothing at all in her hands, and she felt very small indeed before the plunging cow. There was not one thing she could think of to do except run. But she was not in the habit of running, in the first place, and she was not at all sure that she could run faster than the cow anyway. Suppose she went rushing back to the barn. What would she say to her father? What would Henry think of her if she could not bring one single cow in from pasture? And then there was the book which she was to get for doing this one particular thing, in addition to her usual tasks.

Her throat was dry and her knees wobbly, but she took a step toward the cow. No sound came for the words she attempted to say, but she clapped her hands again determinedly. The cow moved to one side skittishly, plunged about once again, and shook her head with big sweeps of her curved horns. But she had moved at least a little away from Anna Elizabeth and in the direction of the barn. And then Anna Elizabeth marched toward her with a resoluteness born of both fury and terror, and the cow gave one final caracole, plunged noisily through the brook, and started for the barn on the run.

Anna Elizabeth's first impulse was to sit down, for she was trembling from head to foot. But she started for the barn at exactly the same pace she had taken coming back. Then she thought of following the fence; instead, she shut her lips in a straight line and walked steadily over the log across the brook. But her mind was not as easily controlled as her body. Over and over again, she kept asking herself *why* the cow had acted that way. Never had she had such an experience before. How was one to know what to expect when things happened like this with no reason or warning at all? Was it something of this kind, happening right out of a clear blue sky, so to speak, that made people believe in magic? The cow simply could not be cross or dangerous, or her father would never ask her to go to the field for her. But if even animals did things because of the control of some certain person who—

The cow settled down to a most sedate and quiet walk before she came to the barnyard. The first sharp flash of lightning cut the heavens as Anna Elizabeth arrived.

"Go to the house then before the rain comes," called her father, who was already milking.

"And what took you so long?" shouted Henry.

"Yes, father," and "Nothing," Anna Elizabeth said by way of reply, and she noticed with a curious kind of objectiveness that the hand that closed the barnyard gate behind her was shaking.

She could ask Henry to go back with her, she

thought, or trade jobs with him perhaps, or ask her father what it was that made cows act in that very unsettling way, or—. She shook her head impatiently and went into the kitchen.

Samuel was scolding a little from his cradle, and Anna Elizabeth went over to pick him up.

"Nothing is wrong with him," said her mother firmly. "Set the table then for supper."

"I can set it with him," said Anna Elizabeth, taking him in her arms. Her hands were still trembling, but she knew well enough what she was doing. You couldn't hold a baby and be afraid, because if you did, the baby would be afraid too.

She set out plates and knives and the spoonholder, and the big salt stand, and dishes of apple butter and preserves. Her mother had the milk and cheese from the spring house. It was dark from the approaching storm, and her mother stopped in her work at the fireplace to light candles. Anna Elizabeth sat down to sing to Samuel.

> When no danger doth appear
>   On the upward way,
> Very wonderful this seems!
>   Still the wise shall say
> Dangers not in evidence
> Do most harm. Have patience!

It was Peter Becker's hymn again, and it might have been written for her, Anna Elizabeth thought. No danger had appeared on her upward way on that particular day, and she evidently was not wise, for she had never once thought about "danger not in evidence." It wasn't a very cheerful idea.

> Very wonderfully God leads thee,
>   No matter what thy part,
> By the desert ways revealing

What is in thy heart.
Trust only his benevolence.
Look to him.   Have patience!

The song might be very true, Anna Elizabeth went
on thinking, but if facing an unruly cow night after
night was a wonderful leading, she couldn't help feeling
that she might dispense with it.

By the desert ways revealing
What is in thy heart.

The desert ways sounded true enough. What was it in
her heart that she would find by walking in desert
ways? There was a sudden sharp flash of lightning, a
crashing of thunder, and the rain began. The only ad-
vantage that Anna Elizabeth could see at this moment
in being frightened so badly by a cow was that she was
taking a violent July thunderstorm with curious calmness.

Anna Elizabeth ate her supper rather quietly. "Father," she said toward the close of the meal, "why don't
we name the cow that won't come up? If I called her
name, do you suppose she would learn to come?"

"What would you name her?" asked Henry.

"Jezebel," said Anna Elizabeth deliberately. "And
we can call her Jezzy for short."

"Why, Anna Elizabeth!" exclaimed her mother.

"She is not wicked," protested Henry.

"Every night someone has to go back for her!" said
Anna Elizabeth. "Would you call that being good?"

"Jezzy," repeated her father, looking quizzically at
his wife. "Well, mother?"

"And what then will our people think?" asked Sister
Landis.

"They will not know it comes from the Bible at all,"
declared Anna Elizabeth. She was thinking of Sister

Frantz and the conversation about Apollos and Apollyon. "The other cows have names."

"Not that kind," said her mother. "You could call her Spotty."

"Jezzy, I think," said Anna Elizabeth firmly.

"Well."

"Why do you keep her, father?" asked Henry. "You might let the church buy her for the Stamms."

"She would be lost all the time then," said Anna Elizabeth, fixing the corners of her mouth exactly the way her father did when he disapproved of something.

"I would not sell to the Stamms what I did not think worth keeping myself, son," said Brother Landis. "But she really is a good cow, the best I have, I think."

Anna Elizabeth thought of the tossing head and plunging hoofs and said words under her breath.

"She is young, and will settle down into a good, obedient cow one of these days," her father went on cheerfully. "And then you children will be glad we kept Jezzy." He smiled at Anna Elizabeth as he used the new name.

But the naming of the cow, although it did relieve Anna Elizabeth's feelings somewhat, did not solve the difficulty she was facing. She got out the inevitable Sunday-school cards after the supper dishes were done and read one after another for a time, sitting as usual on the floor not far from her father's chair. At last she looked up.

"Father, what does the verse from Proverbs mean, the one you asked me to say that night?"

"Perhaps you had better say it again now."

" 'The name of the Lord is a strong tower: the righteous runneth into it, and is safe.' "

"Does the verse help then?"

"All about are dangers many.
To you a castle doth belong;

In God no enemy can spy you,
   Lock yourself in, then, all day long."

"Well?"

"Father, how can a name be a tower? And how can you run into a tower when—" She stopped abruptly. She was about to say, "And how can you run into a tower when what you really have to do is run toward a foolish, galloping cow?" It was all very well to talk about a castle and locking yourself in all day long, but when a cow was to be milked, you just had to bring her up to the barn, that was all.

Her father looked thoughtful, as he so often did over her questions.

"Is that another hard question?" she asked.

"Yes."

"Is it one of those things that Michael says you must find out for yourself?"

"I rather think it is, Anna Elizabeth."

Anna Elizabeth was silent for a few minutes.

"Father, will you go to Germantown next month to get the wheat ground and pick out the book then?" she asked next. "Or will you send some of the wheat to sell with Hans and let him bring the book back?"

Her mother looked up a little anxiously.

"I do not know," her father said slowly. "I will go, I suppose."

"Shoes all around the children must have," said her mother.

Anna Elizabeth frowned a little. "What then has happened since father said the wheat crop was good?"

"Several things there are to buy before the winter sets in, and there is the money for the church fund, and how much did you think a bushel of wheat would bring?"

Anna Elizabeth had no mind for figures, and ordinarily she paid no attention to the price or quantity of wheat. She could do problems as well as Henry, but she simply didn't remember them after she had worked them, even if they concerned the family.

"How much will a book cost?" she asked. "Ten or twelve shillings, not?"

"And what book will you want, then?"

"The *Twice Fifty-Two Bible Stories* maybe?" suggested Anna Elizabeth. "Christopher Sower does not print the *Pilgrim's Progress*."

"And those stories are all in the Bible right now," said her mother. "And a Sower Bible we have."

"Of course," said Anna Elizabeth.

"And not all families have that then," retorted her mother. "A hymnbook we have, and the *ABC Book*, and the Sunday-school cards, and—"

"And I want another," said Anna Elizabeth earnestly. "One for my very own."

"We shall see," said her father. But his voice sounded troubled.

Anna Elizabeth leaned back against the stone fireplace and closed her eyes. Some days were so nice, and some were so decidedly otherwise!

> Keep thy faith and valiance,
> Contend for truth. Have patience!

She was almost angry at the hymn for singing in her mind. She had never very much wanted patience, and tonight she didn't care if she had her "valiance" even. She was only a very tired little girl who felt that something had gone dismally wrong in her little world. Was it possible that her father would not be able to buy a book for her after all? Surely her mother was just feeling worried over something tonight! She did so much want a book!

"By the desert ways revealing—desert ways—desert ways—" She was glad when her mother mentioned bed.

CHAPTER VIII

Brethren Are We

The July newspaper arrived at last, and Hans, red-faced and perspiring, seemed to be in a particularly jolly mood. Anna Elizabeth, forgetting what her mother had said about shoes and thinking only that she would soon have a book of her own to read, no longer cherished any resentment against him, and they had quite a pleasant little talk when his big wagon drove in.

"Ah!" he said, drinking deeply from the spring water Anna Elizabeth brought. "Good this tastes. Soon it will be cider time again, not?"

"Apples are good this year," agreed her father.

"Some cider we will have when you come again," promised Henry, who was then too much fascinated by Hans' horses to pay much attention to the conversation.

"Just talking with Michael I was about a little business matter," Hans told Anna Elizabeth, winking at her father.

"Will you see Michael then when he goes to Germantown?" Anna Elizabeth asked. "Do you live there, Hans?"

A shadow crossed Hans' broad face.

"Well, you see," he said pushing back his cap to scratch his head, "a teamster lives sort of here and there, if you know what I mean. But as for Michael," he went on cheerfully, "don't worry a minute. Keep my eye on that boy I will, sure."

"Michael does not need anybody to watch him," Anna Elizabeth said calmly. "But it would be nice if you went to see him then." She was leafing through the newspaper as she spoke. "Father," she exclaimed in excitement, "here is a new book printed by Christopher Sower. A *German and English Grammar*. Maybe we could get that!"

"No grammar do I want," exclaimed Henry.

"Learn English too, will you?" cried Hans. "And what is this about the book?"

"Father is going to buy me one," said Anna Elizabeth proudly. "One for my very own."

"If we can manage it," her father added. "Go to Germantown I will now whenever I can well get away and see about many little things."

"Last month you should have been there, then," said Hans. "Conrad Beissel and twelve of the Ephrata people were there for a love feast. I did not see them myself, but all the people were talking. Right down through town they walked, and so pale and thin that they might have been ghosts. Men and women both there were."

"Strange," said Brother Landis, shaking his head.

"Strange!" Hans echoed the word explosively, and with a far different emphasis. "I could tell—"

He stopped abruptly and looked down at Anna Elizabeth, who was taking in every word, every inflection of his voice, and every glance. She seemed so alive, so energetic, so curious that it was a pleasure just to look at her.

"And some day to the cloister you will go then, I suppose," he went on, shaking his head mournfully, "and no more freckles on your nose, and no more laughing, and no more good cider and apple pie, and no more arguments with Hans."

Anna Elizabeth looked both astonished and annoyed.

"I go to no cloister," she said with dignity. "Brethren are we."

"And so was Conrad Beissel, I thought," cried Hans.

"But not a good one!"

"Well, very hard it must be to be a good one!" Hans went on. "Ah, these sect people! And have you heard then about the New-Born minister going about farther up the river and yelling so? What next, I should like to know!"

"Well, what about the Lutheran ministers then, I should like to know," cried Anna Elizabeth, thinking of some of the things she had read in the Sower newspaper. "Are they so much better?" She had no intention herself of believing anything the New-Born minister said, but she could not allow Hans to attack all the sect people so. However, Hans went right on talking without even noticing her interruption.

"Always thinking up some new crazy idea about religion, and all the time the French stirring up the Indians in the west, and trouble coming just as sure as I am standing here. Grown men go into cloisters or shout themselves hoarse about visions, and there is the whole west waiting for us to come out and take it!"

"If the sect people who do not believe in fighting were out in the new valleys of Pennsylvania now, no trouble with the Indians would there be," Brother Landis said gravely. "But many and foolish are the ideas

that some men hold, and I do not wonder that a Lutheran thinks so."

"Not about you am I talking," exclaimed Hans,
changing his manner and voice in a moment. "It is as
Anna Elizabeth says, you are different. And Christopher Sower is the best man in all Germantown, that I
will say."

"So he is," cried Anna Elizabeth proudly.

"And no man like him there would be if there was not
perfect freedom in religion," added her father. "So we
get all this other."

"You didn't go out west yet," said Anna Elizabeth.

"Not any more this summer will I go," he replied.
"Maybe not at all. What was it you said about not
turning your back?"

"You can't," said Anna Elizabeth, sighing and
thinking of the obstreperous Jezzy. She looked as if she
would like to say more. "You just can't," she repeated.

"Maybe not," said Hans, shaking his head slowly.
"And what about the wheat then?" he said to Brother
Landis.

Anna Elizabeth went into the house thinking about
all this talk. Hans was very wrong in many of his ideas.
And yet, Anna Elizabeth reflected gravely, she un-
doubtedly liked him better than some Brethren.

Anna Elizabeth's experiences with Jezzy these nights
were troublesome ones. Sometimes Jezzy was in a contrary mood, and she frolicked and plunged until Anna
Elizabeth was as desperate and as terrified as she had
been on the first night Jezzy had acted so. Sometimes
Jezzy fairly came to meet her and walked along to the
barn at a gait so staid and matter-of-fact that Anna
Elizabeth, limp with relief that there had been no scene
on that particular night, was almost as angry as she was
on the other nights for being afraid. Sometimes she
thought Jezzy was only playful; at other times she was
sure the cow was possessed. Over and over again, she

opened her mouth to ask her father about it, but always she changed her mind. More than once she began a conversation with Henry designed to lead up to a discussion of the eccentricities of cows, but never did she get to Jezzy's conduct. Night after night she closed the barnyard gate behind her and walked toward the house, thinking to herself,

> By the desert ways revealing
> What is in thy heart,

and wondering how long she would have to wait to find out anything new and exciting about her own heart. If she once got her book, she thought, perhaps she wouldn't be so afraid.

In the evenings after she had knitted a while, she memorized more texts from the Sunday-school cards, and more of the four-line poems which had been taken from Tersteegen's book of poetry and combined with the Bible verses. Then she would teach words and letters to Catharine and Joanna, and her father would listen to them part of the time, and probably Henry would call out numbers from the cards for her.

And so the weeks went by until late in August her father finally started for Germantown. Not only was he to care for his own affairs; he had the church money and was to bargain for the cow for the Widow Stamm also. Afterwards, she wondered why she should have been so surprised and disappointed upon his return, for she had had warning enough that the book was not a sure and promised thing. But she knew that her father would not even have mentioned it to her unless he was reasonably certain that he could buy it, and her eagerness to own one book, not in partnership with anybody but entirely by herself, overcame her natural shrewdness in guessing just about what the family situation was. When she remembered what her mother had said about the shoes, she drew comfort from the knowledge that her mother was always more cautious about spending money than her father.

Her father left on Wednesday, and he returned the following day. Thursday was a bad day for Anna Elizabeth. In the afternoon she snatched a few moments to look at the Sunday-school cards, and in leafing through the one hundred eighties, she found no 187.

"Mother," she cried, "who then has had the cards since last night?"

Her mother was busily at work out in the yard with the flax, rinsing and bleaching, and Anna Elizabeth knew it was only a few minutes until she would be asked to bring more water.

"The girls had them this morning while you and Henry were in the garden," answered her mother. "Come on then with the pails again."

Anna Elizabeth came out with the cards in her hand instead.

"No 187 is there," she exclaimed. "Where can it be, mother?"

"That I do not know," her mother replied rather sharply. "Put up the cards and come and help. Is this a time to read?"

Anna Elizabeth was leafing through this bunch of ten again. There was no sign of the missing card.

"Anna Elizabeth!"

Anna Elizabeth came up from the spring house with a pail of water.

"Mother, were the girls by the fireplace then?"

Her mother was both busy and tired.

"Now I do not want to hear another word about that!" she said. "Catharine got the cards, and when I saw them I put them back again, but there is no occasion now for a fuss over nothing."

"Nothing!" said Anna Elizabeth bitterly. "And not

even read it, I had! What then may they have done to the two hundreds and the three hundreds?"

"Anna Elizabeth, sometimes—" Her mother set her lips and stopped talking. Anna Elizabeth went for more water.

That night when she went back for Jezzy, there was no cow to be found. She searched the grove of trees and looked at the fence, and finally, finding a place where the rails were not in position, she climbed over and continued her search in a piece of uncleared timber that stretched back beyond the pasture field farther than she liked to think. Henry had milked his cow and come back to hunt for her before she finally found the obnoxious Jezzy, calmly eating grass on new and apparently very satisfactory ground.

"Mother says to hurry in the house and see about the supper," said Henry.

Anna Elizabeth's legs were too tired to hurry very much, but she knew that not ordinarily would Samuel be left with the little girls, and she was worried herself. Her mother was doing most of the milking tonight in the absence of her husband.

In the kitchen Samuel was crying, and the mush was spitting and bubbling in the big iron kettle, and Anna Elizabeth burned her hand hurrying to get the coals brushed off the dutch oven and the biscuits out before they burned. After supper she washed dishes (the soft soap made her hand burn worse than ever), and then she sat down by the fireplace, too tired and excited and uneasy even to read. The little girls were in bed before the sound of her father's wagon came up the lane. Both she and Henry jumped up to run out to meet him, but Anna Elizabeth paused on the steps. She sat down there, feeling suddenly sure that there was no book for her. It wasn't right to want things too much, she felt, and anyone who had set her heart on one certain thing as strongly as she, Anna Elizabeth, had was sure to be disappointed. She slowly went back into the kitchen.

Her father and Henry put the team away before they came in. Brother Landis kissed his wife and then stooped to Anna Elizabeth. The very kindness of his arm around her was confirmation of her fear.

"And so there is no book?"

"Not this time," her father said, speaking with a rather obvious cheerfulness. "Later perhaps—"

"And the shoes?" she asked, looking at her mother.

"Talked to Martin Ritter, I did," said her father, still speaking cheerfully, "and asked him about costs, and he will be going through this neighborhood next month to do the cobbling. If we could mend some old ones now—"

Anna Elizabeth went over to sit on the floor with her back against the fireplace. There were no words to say. She didn't even feel like crying.

"See?" said Henry, coming over beside her and showing her a fine new jackknife. "Much better and bigger it is than the old one!"

So Henry got his knife even though she got no book.

"Anna Elizabeth," said her father, "we really needed another good knife. Henry is old enough to help make many things this winter that we must have, and a knife does not cost so much as a book. You will get your book yet if only you will be patient."

A jackknife was needed! Yes, that was true, and if only she had wanted something useful—needles, a handloom, a pattern for a quilt or a sampler, even, *anything* but a book—she too would have it now. She wished for the moment that she had never learned to read, and now at last she began to cry quietly.

The silence in the kitchen was an unhappy one.

"Anna Elizabeth," said her mother firmly, "more things you have to read than any other girl in the country. And ashamed I would be to act so! Did you—" The last words were addressed to her husband.

"Yes," he replied, sighing. "More it cost than we had thought, but then—"

A sudden suspicion flashed into Anna Elizabeth's mind.

"Not all the people paid their subscription money, I suppose," she exclaimed, "and father bought the cow anyway. And paid more money for it than was promised even! Brother Hammer I think did not give his ten shillings at all!"

"Anna Elizabeth," said her father, very sternly, "Brother Hammer never promised a shilling or even a penny in his life that he did not pay. Do not ever let me hear you speak so again!"

"It was the Kempfers who did not pay," admitted her mother.

"And they have not been to meeting all month," added her father. "So far away they are that we do not know what might have happened. No doubt they will bring their share next month. It is early for farmers to have much money yet anyway. So of course I took from my own money to make up the amount we needed."

"Brethren we are," said Sister Landis, sighing as her husband had done a few minutes before. "There was nothing else to do."

All her life Anna Elizabeth had heard these words, and now she was suddenly angrier than she knew she could be just at the sound of them.

"Yes, Brethren are we," she said between angry sobs, "and so we take care of our cows and the Stamms don't, and they get a new cow, and no book do I have. Brethren are we!"

"Anna Elizabeth!" That was her mother.

"Tired I am of hearing it," she declared, wiping her eyes defiantly. "And it is sorry I am to be born a Brethren! So there!"

"You do not talk to your mother like that, Anna Elizabeth," said her father. "Go to bed now."

"And one is not born a Brethren," added her mother. "Is it Lutherans we are, or Reformed, to be baptizing babies? No one is *born* a Brethren!"

Anna Elizabeth got to her feet and looked from one parent to the other while the force of her mother's words sank into her mind.

"So!" she said slowly, and marched out of the room.

CHAPTER IX

Strange Doctrine

Anna Elizabeth woke up the following morning with eyes that still felt strange and dry from crying the night before. Something had happened, she thought sleepily, as she rubbed her eyes. Then she remembered the book, and she caught her breath in what was half a sob.

She was not at all consistent in her thinking as she lay there reflecting over the whole situation. On the one hand, now that she knew there would be no book, she wasn't really so surprised. Some things were too good to be true, and if she had lived for years with only her *A B C Book* and the Sunday-school cards and the family Bible, she knew perfectly well that she could go on living so. But, on the other hand, she was deeply resentful over her disappointment. If there had been no loss in the church community, and no special subscriptions taken in church, there would have been money for a book, and she knew her father would have bought it gladly. There were so few things that she wanted! One dress after another was made from the same piece of homespun cloth, or from cloth colored with the same homemade dye. When one wore out, or when she outgrew it, she got another. She could see little reason for getting excited over a new dress. Food was always plentiful at their house, but here again it seldom seemed exciting. Even at Thanksgiving time, or Christmas, there were only more pies and cakes, not new ones. When she finished one bit of knitting, there was something else to begin. There was never an end to spinning. She had taken even her experiences with Jezzy with a curious kind of dogged endurance. She knew that life wasn't easy and that some things you simply couldn't escape. And then when she wanted one thing, only one, she didn't get it.

Her mother's words came back to her mind. "One is not born a Brethren!" The idea that she might not join the church when she was older had simply never occurred to her before. Now she saw the matter as something which she herself could decide. Maybe she was never intended to be a Brethren. Maybe that was why she got so angry at people and things. Maybe if she grew up and joined some other church, there would be more books, although no church at all among the German people had a printer so good and so famous as Christopher Sower. But if you weren't all the time giving things to somebody else, maybe you would have more money to buy his books. The Moravians farther up the river had a free school. Perhaps she could be a Moravian and learn to play a trombone. She had heard of organs, but she never hoped to see anything so wonderful as that. There were Mennonites in the neighborhood, too; and if she were a Mennonite, perhaps she could go to Germantown and attend the school of the good Christopher Dock. But her common sense told her that there were plenty of little Mennonite girls growing up in that neighborhood who would never see the school in Germantown and who could not read as well as she could. She sighed. And there was always the settlement at Ephrata. She had told Hans that she would never go to the cloister. But maybe it might be better if she did. There she would always wear the long, white dresses and never have much to eat and never hope for anything at all and so never be unhappy. That might be a better kind of life than the kind she lived, full of curiosity and laughter and eagerness and disappointment and tears.

She must have awakened early, she thought, or her mother would have called her before this. Her mother would not go to Ephrata. What did Maria Christina Sower think about all the day long while her busy husband printed books and mended clocks and made spectacles and compounded medicines and took care of all the German people in the colonies everywhere? She did not think she would go to the cloister. Maybe she would see visions sometime, like Stephen Koch or the New-Born minister, since she certainly could see some things with her eyes shut. And then suddenly for no reason at all she rolled over in bed and began to cry a little again. She didn't want to see visions at all. She only wanted to have one book and to be just an ordinary Brethren all her life. "Very hard it must be to be a good one." So Hans had said, and Anna Elizabeth was very sure that he was right.

At morning prayers her father read Romans 12, and Anna Elizabeth knew well enough why he chose it. Just as if she hadn't heard those words dozens of times before! "Distributing to the necessity of the saints; given to hospitality." There would be something in the prayer along the same line, she felt sure. "For all thy manifold blessings and the innumerable manifestations of thy goodness—" They were manifold all right; Anna Elizabeth wasn't arguing that point, but the fact remained that there was no book in the list of manifestations. She loved her father and her mother and her brothers and sisters, she loved her home and the thousand dear and delightful things that happened there; but she still didn't see any reason in pretending that the situation couldn't be improved.

"Give to us hearts that are full of thy love and mercy, that are grateful for thy goodness, that are willing to share with all thy children." "Even with the Stamms," Anna Elizabeth thought, her eyes tight shut, her mouth in a straight line. Her father's praying often left her in a tumult of conflicting ideas, especially in a time of crisis like this. She believed implicitly in the power of prayer, of course, and she couldn't think of anybody's prayers that would be answered more surely than her father's. And so when he prayed like that, and she was sure he was thinking about her, she felt sometimes as if, with God and her father both concerned about her, she would simply have to be good—she probably couldn't be anything else if she tried. But at other times, reflecting on the perversity of her stubborn little heart, she wasn't sure that even God and her father could make her good! Now and then she wondered if Henry felt the way she did, or Apollonia, or Dorothea, or Michael.

The next days were not too happy. When Anna Elizabeth was feeling gay, her good humor was contagious, and she could make a game out of almost any work. Her sisters would follow her suggestions willingly, and if Henry sometimes made a counter suggestion, almost always a compromise was easily effected. But when Anna Elizabeth was in an angry mood, then no difference how rapidly her hands worked, still things did not go at all well.

Once her mother referred to the book.

"It may be, Anna Elizabeth," she said, "that later in the fall your father can buy a book."

"Later in the fall any extra money must be saved for school," replied Anna Elizabeth briefly, "or there will be no school."

Afterwards she was sorry that she had spoken with

such finality, for her mother said no more about the difficulty, and she herself could not bring up the subject now. Living always with brothers and sisters since the time she could remember, and acknowledging their claim on her time and energy almost from babyhood, she nevertheless was often curiously solitary. For all the questions that she asked, she did a great deal of thinking alone.

August went by, and Jezzy, now wearing a wooden necklace to keep her within bounds, was less fractious than she had been in the previous month. Then came September, with corn cutting and "snitzing" of apples on a large scale, and cider making, and apple-butter boiling. It was at a latter affair that Anna Elizabeth heard more about the Schreibers and their new interest. As usual, Sister Frantz stopped whenever her husband went by or came over to help the Landises, and now she was rushing busily about the big kettle outdoors while Anna Elizabeth was taking a turn at the stirring. Sister Frantz had no baby to keep her at home, as Sister Landis did. It was a late afternoon, and Anna Elizabeth liked the smell of the fire and the haze on the horizon and the great expanse of boiling apple butter, even if her arms were tired.

"Did you hear then last Sunday?" Sister Frantz said to Sister Landis. "Says Sister Schreiber, and if no men then in our church have visions, how can we be sure it is the right one?"

"Tschk!" said Sister Landis. "And there are visions and visions. What kind will satisfy her then?"

Sister Frantz looked a little doubtful.

"Brother Schreiber has the book of Stephen Koch's visions now," she went on, "and they read in it."

"Bought a book?" exclaimed Anna Elizabeth.

"I am not sure where they got it, but they read in it. Very unsettled are they getting, I am thinking."

"I wish I could read it," said Anna Elizabeth.

"Sister Schreiber gave it to me to look at then," admitted Sister Frantz, a little sheepishly. "And I thought maybe your husband would read in it, Mary, and explain it."

"Let me see it," cried Anna Elizabeth, always more curious than afraid. After all, sometime she would have to understand these matters and decide to be a Brethren or something else.

"You cannot stir apple butter and read," replied her mother. "A good thing it is that Brother Duboy is coming over for the next meeting," she went on. "Maybe then he can settle the minds of the people."

"And a strange man he is, too," said Sister Frantz.

"And why then should you say that?" asked her neighbor, a little sharply.

"Never married." Sister Frantz shook her head dubiously. "And an old man now. It is not good for a man to be alone. Why do you suppose he did not go with Conrad Beissel and become a solitary then?"

"Sophia, very foolish are—" Sister Landis took the long-handled stirrer from Anna Elizabeth and spoke to her. "I will stir now. Fix up the fire then for supper."

"Where is the book, Sister Frantz?" Anna Elizabeth asked.

Sister Frantz hesitated.

"Your father will read the book and tell you then if you should read it," her mother declared. "Go now to the kitchen."

On Saturday before the meeting Brother Duboy came to the Landis home. Anna Elizabeth saw him perhaps three or four times a year, and she liked him. That night he and her father talked about the book of visions, and Anna Elizabeth was sorry that she had to be polite and not sit in her favorite place where she could have heard everything. They talked of the New-Born minister too, she was sure.

The following forenoon, when the congregation was

gathered outside in the Schreiber yard and the songs had been sung and Brother Duboy was just getting up to read the scripture, there was a strange interruption.

"And thus saith the Lord," cried a loud voice behind them, "why will ye listen to lies and falsehoods and turn your minds from the truth?"

There was a great rustling as everybody turned around to see who it was that spoke. A rather small man with a thin, stern mouth and piercing eyes was walking straight up in the yard and to the place where Brother Duboy was standing.

"Sent I was to announce unto you the truth, and to free your minds from deception. Hearken now to the words I will speak. And will ye call that a religion that does not free you fully from the power of the devil?"

The New-Born minister, thought Anna Elizabeth. Sent indeed! And the meeting that morning at the Schreibers'!

For five, ten, fifteen minutes the stranger thundered at them his words of truth. Brother Duboy sat down and listened thoughtfully and calmly. Brother Schreiber nodded at intervals and looked at the others triumphantly. Her father sat with his hand over his mouth, and Anna Elizabeth wished that she could know what all he was thinking. Sister Schreiber looked a little nervous, and Sister Frantz seemed quite fascinated. Anna Elizabeth watched the minister intently when she was not watching his audience.

Why did he yell so, she wondered impatiently. Did he really see visions? She did not like the way his thin lips came together. He would not buy books for his daughter, she decided.

When he finally quit talking, Brother Duboy got up again and again opened his Bible.

"Brethren, the lesson this morning is from the fourth chapter of 1 Timothy," he began, just as if nothing had happened to interrupt him. "Let us all give ear unto the word of the Lord."

But the stranger started off down the road as dramatically as he had appeared.

"Let us all attend unto the reading of God's word," Brother Duboy repeated, calmly and deliberately.

"But when the spirit bids go again, his servant can tarry not," cried the strange preacher.

They listened to him, thought Anna Elizabeth indignantly, and now he would not listen to them. Afraid perhaps!

" 'Now the Spirit speaketh expressly, that in the latter times some shall depart from the faith,' " read Brother Duboy, " 'giving heed to seducing spirits, and doctrines of devils.' "

Anna Elizabeth stole a look at Brother Schreiber to see how he was taking this. That man a minister! From all the little remarks and snatches of conversation that she had been able to pick up, he shouted and gestured and shut his eyes at times just the way Conrad Beissel did when he preached and fascinated some people so.

" 'Speaking lies in hypocrisy; having their conscience seared with a hot iron—' "

Anna Elizabeth thought of the last time she had burned her hand and felt the vigor of the metaphor.

" 'Forbidding to marry, and commanding to abstain from meats, which God hath created to be received with thanksgiving—' "

What did Conrad Beissel think when he read those words, she wondered. He with his solitary brethren and sisters, and eating no pork! It was strange how many curious ideas people got when they tried to preach, she thought. Maybe it would be better to be a Lutheran and not try to preach until some person very high in authority had told you what to believe, and then you wouldn't have all these silly ideas. Hans had no silly ideas, but Anna Elizabeth doubted if he read his Bible very often. On the other hand, Christopher Sower read his own Bible, she knew. And her father had said that to have a Christopher Sower, you had to have all these others.

When she began listening again, Brother Duboy was reading. " 'But refuse profane and old wives' fables, and exercise thyself rather unto godliness.' " And that was the text from which he preached. Anna Elizabeth listened to him gladly.

After church, Michael talked with her a little.

"Sorry I am about the book," he said.

There wasn't anything to say in reply to this. She asked a question instead.

"You will be a Brethren some day, Michael?"

"Yes."

"And I?"

"Why, yes!"

"But, Michael, I can see with my eyes shut!" she reminded him. "Perhaps—" It was very difficult to put into words what she wanted to say.

"Now, look, Anna Elizabeth," said Michael, making a very long speech for him. "Very foolish it would be never to shut the eyes and see things in the dark. But very foolish it would be never to open them and see whether one remembered rightly and to learn new things."

"That's what Hans means when he talks so about Conrad Beissel and his followers shutting themselves up in a cloister and not knowing about the Indians or anything, isn't it?" she asked.

"Yes."

Anna Elizabeth changed the subject suddenly.

"You remember when I was wondering about the name Apollonia?" she said. "It was when your mother was at our house, and I suppose she told you."

Michael nodded.

"Well, there is an Apollonia in the Bible, but it is a

place and not a person. 'Now when they had passed through Amphipolis and Apollonia, they came to Thessalonica.' Do you suppose Apollonia was named from that verse?"

"I do not know."

"And there is an Apollyon, too, in Revelation. I guess the Apollyon in *Pilgrim's Progress* was named for the one in the Bible. Michael, sometimes I think everything's in the Bible!"

"Yes?" Michael smiled at the warm brown eyes looking into his. "But I do not think you need to worry about anything, Anna Elizabeth," he said, going back to the earlier topic of conversation. "You will not keep your eyes shut."

"No." And Anna Elizabeth's sigh was a curious mixture of relief and resignation. "I guess it is Brethren I am."

CHAPTER X

The Husbandman Waiteth

When the meeting was over that Sunday Brother Duboy came home again with the Landises, and while her father and Henry were doing the evening chores, Anna Elizabeth saw him standing quite alone in the yard, looking toward the west and apparently watching the sun go down, just as she so often did. She wanted very much to talk to him, but she was not quite sure that he would be interested in her questions. Peter Becker she would have gone to without hesitation, but he had children and grandchildren, and Abraham Duboy didn't. She remembered Sister Frantz's words about him and tried to imagine, as she did occasionally, what life at Ephrata must be like. Sister Frantz thought it strange that he had not gone there. What was it that made people leave their families and go to live as solitary brethren or sisters? Brother Duboy had never married, but he was dressed just like any other man in the church, and he had no queer ideas about what to eat. He did not look as if he saw visions, either; he just looked like a very interesting man with whom she could discuss any number of questions. Now she stood by the front door steps, irresolute. After all, he was sixty-eight years old, and she was only twelve. Perhaps he would rather go on thinking than be bothered. And then he turned and saw her.

"A nice evening," he said to her, smiling.

"Yès," she said, smiling shyly in return.

"You listened very well this morning," he went on, "to both sermons."

Anna Elizabeth looked surprised. She did not suppose that he had noticed her.

"I liked your sermon." Anna Elizabeth still spoke hesitantly, uncertain whether to begin talking in earnest with this man or not.

"And not the other?" There was a kind of half twinkle in Brother Duboy's eyes as he said this that reminded Anna Elizabeth of her father. Perhaps he had watched her during the service that morning and guessed her thoughts just as she loved to watch other people and try to think what was going on in their minds. She decided that she could trust this man.

"Brother Duboy," she said, going directly to the matter that bothered her, "how can you be sure then that the minister's visions this morning were not true?"

"Did I say they weren't true?" he asked, and she felt his eyes, keen and kindly, searching her face.

"No," she said, "but you didn't believe them, and neither did father."

"Well, Anna Elizabeth, I don't believe a true vision, one that helps either the person who receives it or anybody else, comes to anyone unless that person is exercising in godliness. You remember the sermon? And I am quite sure that a true vision would not contradict the Bible. So when a man says he has had a vision, I would listen very carefully to what he said, and remember the Word, and look to see how he lived."

"Is the New-Born minister not a good man? Perhaps he has been over where you live?"

Brother Duboy hesitated.

"I thought he was not," said Anna Elizabeth, interpreting Brother Duboy's silences as easily as she did her father's. "What about Stephen Koch's visions then?"

Again Brother Duboy hesitated. "Very sincere are many of the Ephrata people, no doubt, but—"

"Michael thinks they keep their eyes shut and see visions too much when they should keep their eyes open most of the time."

"Michael is a wise boy," replied Brother Duboy, smiling.

"And I should not read Stephen Koch's visions then?" Anna Elizabeth asked doubtfully. She had not yet asked her father about the book.

Abraham Duboy kept on smiling.

"Sometime you will read the book, I think, Anna Elizabeth. And when you do, or when you read any other book like that, you will ask yourself, What then does this tell me that is not already in the Bible? and then, Do these new things help me at all to be a Christian? You will remember? The Bible is a very *helpful* book, Anna Elizabeth, not just unusual and interesting."

"Yes." Anna Elizabeth thought about the verse which said the name of the Lord was a strong tower and wondered if she should ask Brother Duboy about it. But he would probably answer her just the way her father had done. "And I thought while this stranger was preaching this morning that he would not buy a book for his daughter," she said, by way of concluding the discussion.

"Ah, yes, your father was telling me about the book," said Brother Duboy.

Anna Elizabeth was on the defensive immediately. What had her father been telling Brother Duboy?

"He said how well you can read and write and how sorry he was that he could not bring you a new book this fall."

Anna Elizabeth looked down, very much ashamed of her sudden anger. She might have known that her father would say only good things about her—how well she could read, not how angry and unhappy she got over her disappointment.

"A good thing it is to read," went on Brother Duboy, "and a fortunate girl you are to have so much —the Sower Bible, and the *A B C Book* and the hymnbook and the Tersteegen cards. And there is the newspaper every month, and the almanac every year."

"Yes," said Anna Elizabeth, "but—"

"A marvelous thing is printing then. 'By it he being dead yet speaketh.'"

"Yes," said Anna Elizabeth again, "but I wanted—" And then, very much to her own astonishment, she began to cry. She had thought she was through crying about the book long ago.

"Now then," said Brother Duboy in a voice so kind that Anna Elizabeth kept on crying, "sit down here on the steps, we will, and you will tell me all about it." He led her over to the steps, and they sat down together, and he patted with a kindly old hand first the white cap over the red-brown hair and then the blue-clad shoulder beside him. "You wanted a book for yourself only?"

"So I did, and I would have it now, only father helped to buy the cow for the Stamms," she said.

"Well, of course, Anna Elizabeth, that was right, you know. We cannot let our Brethren go hungry, and they had no other cow."

"Brethren are we," quoted Anna Elizabeth bitterly through her tears.

"So we are," said Brother Duboy firmly.

"But you don't understand," said Anna Elizabeth, saying at last the things she had been thinking for weeks. "*Always* is there something going wrong at the Stamms'. Last summer the pigs got into their garden, and take them things all summer we did. And they never get any really good thread from their flax, and their soft soap never turns out right, and their apple butter always scorches. *Always* we must be doing something for them. Night after night I go back after Jezzy, and—"

"Jezzy?"

"Our newest cow. Named for Jezebel in the Bible she is, too, and I named her, because she never will come up with the others or do what she is supposed to. Frightens me out of my wits she does, but I take care of her, and why then could not George Stamm take care of one cow? He does not want to learn to read, and because he does not do so well even as Henry then at taking care of things, no book do I get."

"Anna Elizabeth," said Brother Duboy gravely, "your father and mother did not tell you such things about the Stamms."

"As if one knows then only the things that someone tells him!" exclaimed Anna Elizabeth, beginning to cry again. In spite of the shadow of a smile that crossed Brother Duboy's face, she still felt somehow sure that he was sympathetic, and she had not cried for months with the complete satisfaction and abandon that she now felt. It was so seldom that you found a person who did not tell you right away to quit. She was telling Brother Duboy things that she had not even told her father.

"You will always know a great many things that no one tells you," agreed Brother Duboy, still speaking gravely, "and so you must learn hard lessons while you are still a little girl. Food is more important than books."

"Oh, but it isn't!" protested Anna Elizabeth.

"You say that because you have never been hungry," replied Brother Duboy. "One does not *like* food as well as books, or think about it as much, but it must come first. Suppose you had nothing at all to eat for a whole day? Or a week?"

Anna Elizabeth tried to think. Food to her meant stirring and turning things over a hot fireplace and scouring heavy kettles and pans afterward. Of course there was the sound of ham sizzling in the skillet and the smell of fresh bread coming out of the oven and the perfectly delicious taste of deep-dish apple pie. If you never had any of those things, if you had nothing at all to eat—

"Suppose you did not eat for a month? Or two? You would die, Anna Elizabeth."

"Yes," she said.

"Now suppose you did not see a book or read a word for a day, what would happen? Or for a week?"

"Nothing," admitted Anna Elizabeth.

"Or a month? Or a year? Or five years, even? Would you then not want to read any more?"

Again Anna Elizabeth tried to think. A month wouldn't make any difference, and she really didn't think a year would. There was not always a schoolteacher in the winter months, and she didn't forget what she had learned before. She could repeat her Bible verses and practice her writing even if she had no book at all. If she waited five years, she would be as old as Michael, and ready to join the church. But her father had remembered the stories from *Pilgrim's Progress* much longer than five years even, and he still said them, using almost exactly the same words every time.

"Some people are born with a love of books, it

seems, and very early they learn to read. So is Anna Elizabeth. Some people learn very slowly, but a little do they learn eventually if they live long enough. So perhaps is this George Stamm. But all people must eat, or no chance will any of them have to learn what God gives them the ability to learn. So when people are hungry, the Brethren give them food, and they do not ask how much they have read or even how good they are. If a person does not have food, how then can he learn to be good and do the will of God?"

Anna Elizabeth was looking up at him very seriously and thinking hard.

"But—"

"People cannot wait for food. There will always be books."

The phrase caught her imagination and sang in her mind.

"Always?" she asked earnestly.

"Always."

"For me, Anna Elizabeth?"

Brother Duboy smiled and spoke without hesitation.

"Most particularly for you, Anna Elizabeth."

There was no reason at all for it, but Anna Elizabeth started to cry softly.

"Very hard it is to wait," she said.

"Very hard," agreed Brother Duboy. And then suddenly the gentle old man who had been so close to her and so completely understanding of her difficulties seemed far away. He looked across the cleared fields to the soft glow above the trees where the sun had gone down. "It is the things we want most that we can wait for longest. 'Behold, the husbandman waiteth for the precious fruit of the earth, and hath long patience for it, until he receive the early and latter rain. Be ye also patient.' "

Anna Elizabeth forgot about herself in an eager attempt to understand the man who had been so understanding of her. What was it that Brother Duboy wanted? Was it possible that something as precious to him as any book was to her he still was waiting for? What did he see as he looked across the gently rolling countryside? The fields around Epstein, Germany, perhaps, where he had grown up, and something that he had wanted when he was only as old as Michael.

" 'The husbandman—waiteth—long—' " He repeated the words almost in a whisper as he got slowly to his feet.

Anna Elizabeth also stood up. She saw the road and the fields and the woods beyond only dimly, but her voice was steady when she spoke again.

"Yes, Brother Duboy," she said. "And I too can wait."

CHAPTER XI

Desert Ways

October came, and corn husking, and the gathering of pumpkins and squashes, and then November, and butchering, and the genuine approach of winter. The winter itself seemed long to Anna Elizabeth. School and church were interrupted by heavy snows, and by the time March winds began to blow, Anna Elizabeth found herself often strangely tired. The food seemed tasteless, and the plates and kettles heavier than ever to wash. Samuel was walking all around now, and had to be watched every minute that he was not held or tied in a chair. Henry had proved himself remarkably adept with his jackknife during the winter, and he had had so much honest pleasure in what he made that Anna Elizabeth had long ago ceased to feel regretful over the gift that he had received when she had failed to get hers. There was almost no end to the useful and even necessary things a boy could make with a knife—clothespins, hinges, buttons for closing doors, butter paddles, axe helves, shingles. The latter had a money value, and often men and boys split and smoothed them during the winter to sell in the spring. Anna Elizabeth had known all this when her father brought the knife for Henry and not the book for her, but she realized the truth of it more than ever that winter while she watched Henry work with something of an adult's energy and faithfulness. She was very glad now that she had cherished no resentment, for he was whittling when she was not around, and saying mysterious things about her birthday.

"A surprise you will have," he told her. "In fact, if father will help me a little, *two* surprises."

"Shall I guess?"

"You could not *ever* guess the one," Henry told her with enormous satisfaction. "Not even you could guess this!"

After the snows came the mud, and when Hans came one day in the middle of March, he had two papers with him, although not the one for March 16.

"Where have you been?" cried Anna Elizabeth, running out between puddles of melting snow to carry in the papers. "Mother says to come in for a little while and hot cider we will have."

"Such mud!" cried Hans. "You should see the road between Germantown and Philadelphia! It is one swamp!"

"How is the road to the blacksmith shop?" asked her father. "No farther than that will I go now, but I should go there."

"Another day or two and it will not be so bad," replied Hans. "Cider, did you say?"

They started toward the kitchen.

"A message I have for you," said Hans to Anna Elizabeth suddenly. He set down the huge mug into which Anna Elizabeth had poured the cider. "Suppose I should have forgotten!"

"For me? And who then that you see do I know?"

"In Germantown? Who indeed!" Hans looked at

Henry and her father in mock surprise. "Who does she know in Germantown?"

"Michael," cried Anna Elizabeth, smiling in delight. "Did you talk with him, Hans?"

"Well he is, and learning his weaving beautifully, and earning a little money besides. And I said to him only a few days ago, what words do I take then to the red-headed little girl on the Manatawny? Very angry she gets sometimes, but when she smiles, she smiles all the way from her brown eyes right down to her dancing feet."

"Oh-h-h!" Anna Elizabeth looked at her mother a little uneasily, for none of the plain people danced. It was a strange word in their home.

"Not dancing like the Philadelphia and Germantown ladies do," said Hans, rather hastily, "although you could do that too well enough, I have no doubt. But your feet and hands are never quiet, and you smile more with your eyes than most people can when they use all their face then."

Anna Elizabeth thought that Hans knew nothing at all of how she had been feeling these last weeks or he would not have talked so.

"What did Michael say to all this foolish talk?" she asked, her hands raised in quick deprecation.

"He said, like a grave and sober member of a grave and sober people, that he sent his greetings to Anna Elizabeth and all the Landises, and he hoped to see you before so long maybe."

"Member?"

"Baptized he was while Peter Becker was there for a meeting, I heard. And he says it is true."

"Very good that is," said her father, smiling.

"Yes? Well, probably so." And Hans patted the heads of Catharine and Joanna, chirruped to Samuel, and left in a burst of unusual good cheer, even for him.

The girls rushed to the window to watch the team leave.

"Dancing!" said Sister Landis to no one in particular.

"It is not dancing my feet are these days, mother," said Anna Elizabeth, thinking how often she had felt tired during the month.

"And what then is wrong with you, Anna Elizabeth?" asked her mother anxiously. "Is it not well you are?"

"Tired," said Anna Elizabeth. She stood a moment thinking of that peculiar feeling she had. But there wasn't really anything to say more than she had said, and so she only repeated the word, with a sigh. "Tired."

"I do not know why you should be tired," said her mother. "I will get out the herbs. Some pennyroyal, perhaps, or sassafras. You are not too tired to read?"

Anna Elizabeth put down the paper that she had picked up. "What is there to do, mother?" she asked.

A few days later, Brother Landis went to the blacksmith shop and took Henry with him. Anna Elizabeth watched them drive away with a strange, uneasy feeling. There had been several unusually mild days, and so the time seemed an opportune one. But not long after they left that afternoon it turned cloudy, and Anna Elizabeth, pausing in the intervals of her work to look out the window and down the road which they had traveled, felt the air grow colder and the wind rise. When she last noticed the cows in the barnyard, they stood huddled near to the barn to get away from the cold wind, and she afterwards wondered why she had not gone out then to put them in the barn. Toward evening it grew astonishingly cold and stormy. When the rain finally began, it beat against the windows and the wind howled down the chimney with unusual force.

"Your father is late," Sister Landis said, watching

the rain. "Others perhaps came to the shop today, too, and the blacksmith was busy."

"Yes," said Anna Elizabeth. Samuel was very heavy in her arms as she walked about setting the table for supper.

"Lights we must have already, Anna Elizabeth. Early it is for that."

"I'm hungry," said Catharine. "I want a piece, mother."

"I'm hungry, I'm hungry, I'm hungry." Joanna took up the cry with wailing persistence.

"Now wait a few minutes we will yet for your father," declared their mother. "Oh, I almost forgot the cows. We should have done the milking tonight, no difference what he said. Go and turn them in this minute, Anna Elizabeth. They should not be out in the storm."

"Yes, mother." Anna Elizabeth stood still a moment, holding the baby.

"Put him in the cradle then, and Catharine must see that he stays there," said her mother. "He does not need to be held all the time. Catharine must learn to watch him."

It had been a "tired" day for Anna Elizabeth, and she moved slowly in the direction of the cradle. Her mother looked at her inquiringly. Samuel raised his voice in healthy protest at being put in so close and uninteresting a place, and Anna Elizabeth's hands moved slowly as she tied him firmly in a sitting position. He was so active that he needed watching even when so placed. Then she put on her coat and hood and mittens. She paused with her hand on the door, hearing Samuel's cries and seeing her mother's face flushed with the heat as she bent over the boiling kettle. She did not want to go out.

"Anna Elizabeth, are you sick?" asked her mother,

looking up in surprise. Anxiety made her voice sharp. It was unusual for her daughter to be so slow.

Anna Elizabeth wished that she knew. Was it being sick when a person simply ached all over, not anywhere in particular, but just mostly all over? She couldn't think of any way to explain how she felt. She was tired, and picking up one foot and then the other was an effort. Ordinarily she was so well and so active that she could not understand at all her present feelings. If you burned your finger, you felt pain, but this—. So she only shook her head in answer to her mother's question and opened the door.

The wind blew in with a *whoosh* that set the candles flickering clear across the room, and Anna Elizabeth hastily closed it behind her. As she stepped into the yard and away from the protection of the house, the full force of the gale caught her. She was amazed at its power. Ordinarily she didn't mind pitting her own strength against a storm, and now she tightened her lips and stiffened her body to meet the fury of the wind. But with her first steps she made another discovery. It was rain unmistakably that beat against her cheeks and cut through her wool stockings, but it was ice that she was walking on. With every step her foot sank through a thin layer of it, and then she had to pull her foot out before she could step again.

She was breathless when she reached the barn. Quickly she opened the door for the cows to come in, and then leaned back against the wall, shivering and trying to regain her breath. She had closed the lower part of the door when she noticed something. Jezzy was gone. She shut her eyes, then opened them. No, there was no Jezzy. She looked out the upper part of the stable door. She couldn't be certain, but even through the rain she thought she saw a place in the fence that showed what had happened. She was perfectly sure that earlier in the afternoon Jezzy had become bored with the barnyard, and that since the wooden yoke had been put away during the winter months, she had gone over the fence and was even then hidden in her favorite clump of trees at the far end of the pasture field.

There was no use in wondering what to do. The answer to that question was unmistakable. A dozen things could happen to make her father and Henry late, and the storm would grow worse during the night, not better. They were not the sort of people who left their stock out in a storm to get lost or sick from exposure. But for no good reason at all, Anna Elizabeth now saw Jezzy as she had looked that first July evening when Anna Elizabeth had been frightened by her skittish behavior. She felt the old terror, and the weakness in her knees, and the dryness in her throat, and the sick feeling in the pit of her stomach. In addition to that, she was very cold, and very tired, and very miserable. She simply would *not* go back in the field for Jezzy on a night like this. She leaned against the stable door, sobbing a little in pure wretchedness. It would be so easy to be like the Stamms!

Then she went out the door, closing it carefully behind her, picked her way across the barnyard, and opened the gate into the lane. And so through the dark and the wind and the rain she started her journey.

So far as her body was concerned, there was only one thing to do: pick up with conscious effort from the layer of ice one foot and then the other, and keep going. The wind was at her back, and that helped a little. But the tiredness in her legs soon became an ache that she could have told her mother about with no difficulty, and she grew chilled to the bone. As for her mind, there seemed nothing to do about that. It took all her energy to keep her feet moving, and so there seemed to be no end to the ideas that went round and round in her mind.

Why did she keep on going when she was so tired

and afraid? Was it because she, like Apollyon, had no
armor for her back? Who would bring her the leaves
from the tree of life if she really was getting sick? What
had happened to the poor old woman with the piercing
black eyes? Was it possible that her glance could have
anything at all to do with Jezzy's unreasonable behavior, or her own fright, or weariness? Suppose she
should see a vision? Anything might appear out of this
storm, even though her eyes were wide enough open. It
was difficult to see through the dusk and rain even
when she tried ever so hard. But suppose that hidden in
the clump of trees should be, not Jezzy, but—pick up
one foot, pick up the other! It would probably be Jezzy
in the clump of trees, shaking her head with great
sweeps of her horns, and then what would she do? Run
into the tower, or lock herself into a castle all day long,
perhaps!

She kept rather close to the fence, because she
wasn't even sure the log was still over the creek, and if
it was, it would be too icy to walk. Her feet were wet
long before she crossed the creek, and so wading that
was a minor matter. She was surprised at how much
water there was, though. She was surprised, too, at how
fiercely the wind pushed her, and she wondered how
she could ever get back, especially if Jezzy was not in
the mood to go.

At last she came to the clump of trees. She opened
her mouth to call, but she could only cling to the first
tree and try to regain her breath. Jezzy must have
sensed her approach, for without waiting for a word of
any kind, she came out from the far corner and went
straight toward Anna Elizabeth with an apologetic
moo. She seemed positively grateful for company.
Anna Elizabeth knew that she should feel thankful and
relieved; actually she felt only incredibly tired. She put
her arm around Jezzy's neck, and they started back for
the barn.

The wind now hit her straight in the face, and she wondered if she could have faced it if she were not clinging fast to Jezzy. Down into the ice, getting harder every moment, went her feet; straight into her face came the cold rain, blinding her eyes and stinging her cheeks; always there was the wind, blowing her skirts about and penetrating through every garment she was wearing. Jezzy was now leading. She hit the brook farther down at a place more in line with the lane, and Anna Elizabeth felt the force of the water, higher than it had been when she crossed, and was splashed to her knees as Jezzy plunged noisily through. Now it was hard to keep up with Jezzy, for the cow was increasing her speed as she got nearer to the barn. It was hard, too, to keep her feet out of the way of the cow's, and desperately hard to pick them up at all. The warm fireplace danced before her eyes, and she heard Samuel crying, and the girls asking for food. They were sitting around the fire right now, no doubt, and eating something, and Henry might be in the cold rain, but at least he could get under the cover of the wagon somewhat and he was with his father. She seemed utterly alone, in a desert of blinding rain and icy terrain, but she was beginning not to care very much. Her feet felt numb, and the shadowy outlines of the farm buildings swam before her eyes, and her head felt far too large and very strange.

> By the desert ways revealing
> What is in thy heart.

How very strange, she thought in a last coherent moment, to call all this rain and ice and cold a *desert!* There wasn't anything in her heart except love for books—that seemed a very long time ago—and a fear of Jezzy—but that was gone—and an incredible tiredness.

And now they had reached the short lane, and the barnyard gate was very near. Jezzy gave a triumphant lunge, broke away from Anna Elizabeth, and rushed toward the barn. Anna Elizabeth knew that something had happened, and for a moment she kept a dizzy, uncertain balance in the wind and rain. Then nothing at all mattered, and there was only blackness, an overwhelming, blessed blackness.

CHAPTER XII

There Will Always Be Books

The next days were always very vague in Anna Elizabeth's mind. Somebody, it seemed, was always giving her something to drink, and she wondered why there should be chicken broth so long. It couldn't be Sunday every day. Once she was sure that Sister Frantz was sitting by her bed, and she tried hard to think how that could be.

"Now just go back to sleep," said Sister Frantz crooningly. "A sick girl you are, and sleep is what you need."

Sick, thought Anna Elizabeth curiously. But then Sister Frantz sometimes got things mixed up, and so she dismissed the matter, and drifted back into the restful blackness.

Another time she heard Samuel crying. There was no mistaking that hearty sound, and in a flash the lighted kitchen came back, and her mother near the fireplace, and the little girls begging for food, and Samuel crying in his cradle. She opened her eyes and saw only her mother.

"Where is Samuel?" she asked, and although it made no sense at all, she was almost sure that her mother started to cry. It was much too difficult to fit such confusing impressions together to make a coherent story; it was much pleasanter just to lie very still and let everything get black again.

Pleasantest of all the memories of those few days was the recollection of her mother singing. Sometimes she was too hot to rest comfortably, and then there would be something to drink, perhaps, and a hand on her forehead, and her mother's voice singing just as she did to Samuel in the middle of the night. It gave Anna Elizabeth an altogether delightful feeling, as if she were only a very little girl indeed, with no tasks to do or things to learn, and nothing in the world to think about even, except to lie still and let someone else take care of her. It made her realize somehow that once she had been a tiny baby, being cared for, and not taking care of someone else.

And then one morning she woke up just as naturally as could be and saw to her great surprise that she was in the downstairs bedroom. Her first impulse was to call, but instead she looked around. There was water on a little table near her bed, and a jar of some peculiar looking stuff, and a teaspoon. She sat up in bed, but she felt lightheaded in that position, and so she lay down again quickly.

Soon her mother came in. At first she did not speak; she only stroked her daughter's forehead and then patted her hand. Anna Elizabeth felt very strange.

"Was I sick, mother?" she asked.

Her mother nodded. "But much better you are now."

And then her father came in. Had he heard her voice? He looked at her strangely too, and after a moment he smiled.

"So," he said, and put his arm around his wife. "Better she is this morning?"

"When did you come home, father?" asked Anna Elizabeth.

Her mother started stirring with the things on the little table. "We will take this now," she said, "and talk later." She held out a spoonful of something.

"From the good Christopher Sower then, father?" asked Anna Elizabeth, smiling and thinking of the Lehmans. She knew well enough that there were always a few medicines in the house from this one shop in Germantown.

Her father nodded, but his smile seemed not so gay as she expected.

"Shall I get up now?" she inquired next, a little doubtfully.

"No, indeed," exclaimed her mother quickly.

"I think she can sit up in bed for her birthday," said her father cheerfully.

"Birthday!" Anna Elizabeth did some quick figuring.

"And do I not have a daughter who is thirteen on the twenty-sixth day of March, 1748?" asked her father.

"Yes," she said. If they didn't want to talk, she would just lie still, and sooner or later she would have the whole story thought out. The children came in quietly a little later, and Henry told her that Jezzy was as fine as could be.

"She got over the fence, didn't she?" asked Anna Elizabeth, and Henry nodded and said that it was fixed now.

"Sister Frantz was here all night once and most of one day," said Catharine, "and mother stayed up with you one night, and father one night."

"Girls tell everything!" said Henry in disgust.

"Did someone stay up with me three nights?" Anna Elizabeth asked.

Henry nodded. "Most of the time. But we weren't

going to tell you right away. Mother doesn't want you to worry."

"Do you girls want to say your letters and words in here?" asked Anna Elizabeth. "Or is it too cold when you are not in bed?"

"Mother said not yet for a day or two," Catharine replied.

"It isn't very cold out," Henry added. "The ice lasted only a day, and father has kept a big fire in the fireplace ever since you were in here."

The following day her father and mother both came into her room quite early.

"So she slept the whole night through," said her father, smiling.

"True." There was one more thing Anna Elizabeth wanted to know. "Where did you find me, father? I can't remember getting to the barnyard at all."

"About halfway up the lane." He paused, then leaned over and spoke to her very earnestly and gently. "Anna Elizabeth, why did you go back? Certainly you know that not all the cows in the colony are worth as much as our little girl. Why did you go back when you were feeling so bad?"

Anna Elizabeth felt the tears coming to her eyes. When someone spoke to her in a voice as kind as that, she had no defense. But she swallowed and answered with just a trace of mischief.

"Brethren are we. If we do not take care of our cows, then, father, who will subscribe for the poor in the church?"

The expression on her father's face was so puzzling that she was almost sorry she had said this.

"Brethren we are, that is true," he said at last, "and proud I am of my little daughter. But you must never do anything like that again, Anna Elizabeth, without first asking your mother. Do you promise? We cannot have a girl who is sick starting off on a chase after a foolish cow."

The tears were in Anna Elizabeth's eyes again.

"There won't be another time like that," she said. Her father looked so concerned over her that she finally made an attempt to explain. "You see, I was afraid."

"Afraid of Jezzy?" asked her father.

Anna Elizabeth nodded, feeling very small indeed.

"And you were afraid last summer too?"

Again Anna Elizabeth nodded.

"But there was nothing to be afraid of," said her mother, looking at her husband for confirmation.

"No, mother." It was strange how people told you things after you had found them out for yourself. "I'm not afraid now."

"And so you found the strong tower?" asked her father, stooping to kiss her.

"I—I don't know, father. Maybe I did."

Later in the day her mother went back to that same evening.

"Anna Elizabeth, why didn't you tell me at least how you felt when I asked you to put the cows in?"

"Mother, there wasn't anything to tell," said Anna Elizabeth helplessly. "I never felt that way before. How could I know I was getting sick then?"

"But you did not feel like going out."

"Often I do not feel like doing things," said Anna Elizabeth honestly. "And you were busy, and the cows had to be turned in."

She knew intuitively something of what was in her mother's mind. She was sure her mother was regretting her occasional sharpness of speech. But she was not angry or displeased with her mother at all. In fact, as she lay there in bed she thought of how her mother sat by the fireplace night after night, always spinning or knitting while her father read, and she decided that it was harder to be a woman than to be a man. She would grow up to be like her mother after all, she felt, and she too would knit and spin sometime while her husband taught little boys and girls to read. She would rather have been a schoolmistress in Philadelphia, but she wasn't a Quaker, and she would probably marry just as her mother had done. But not either of the Hammer boys or George Stamm! She was defiant on that point, even after her illness.

However, it was impossible to say all these things. And so it was something of a relief when the sounds of chattering and then of exclamation from the kitchen rose to a climax and Catharine ran into the room.

"Samuel is choking," she cried.

Her mother rushed to the kitchen. Anna Elizabeth sat up in bed anxiously and listened. There were thumps and strangled sounds and excited questions, and then a series of loud yells from Samuel.

"Mad only he is now," thought Anna Elizabeth, and she lay down again. Very hard was the life of a woman!

Anna Elizabeth decided to have her presents on the afternoon of her birthday. So after dinner the family gathered in the room where she still was in bed, although propped up now with pillows. Henry's came first, a handloom which he had made almost entirely by himself.

"Father helped me burn the holes in it," he said.

There was a new dress from her mother to be worn on Sundays that summer. And there was quite a large package to be opened. Henry untied strings and the girls folded up the paper. Anna Elizabeth opened the box and saw within two books. She was quite speechless.

"Take them out," cried Henry, "and see who they are from!"

"Father," said Anna Elizabeth at last, "there was no money for books."

"We sold the shingles, didn't we, father? And I helped make them too, with my knife. Hans took them when he was here the last time."

Anna Elizabeth took out the first book. It was the *German and English Grammar*. She turned it around and around, still finding no words with which to say thanks.

"And look at the other too," cried the irrepressible Henry.

She lifted it out. It was the *Pilgrim's Progress*. She looked around from one to another. Her mother was smiling, her father fairly beaming.

"Why don't you talk?" asked Catharine with interest.

"Look inside," said her father. "I did not buy you two books. But I will read them," he added.

Anna Elizabeth smiled at him. Inside the cover was a name she had never seen before, but under it was hers, Anna Elizabeth Landis, and under that the words, "From Michael Frantz."

"Michael could not buy a book, father," she exclaimed.

"Hans got it for him," cried Henry, simply bursting with his story. "Got it for only a little bit of money, Michael says. Don't you remember when you asked Hans to read the book for you and he wouldn't?"

"Michael was here that day, you remember," explained her father, "and he asked Hans about it then. I told Henry last fall when I couldn't buy the book for you. Didn't you notice how Hans grinned and winked when he was here the last time then?"

"I was too tired, I guess," said Anna Elizabeth. "But who brought the books here?" she asked suddenly.

"Michael came home and brought them. He left them here last night," said her mother.

"And he was very quiet so that you wouldn't hear," said Henry. "Aren't you pleased?"

Anna Elizabeth could only nod. *Two* books!

"Can we play with the Sunday-school cards any time we want to now?" asked Catharine.

Her father put a quiet hand on her shoulder and smiled.

"You will learn your words, but not play all the time you want to, perhaps," he said. "Do you want to begin reading now, Anna Elizabeth?"

Anna Elizabeth shook her head. "I just want to think," she said.

But the family had only begun to scatter when there was the sound of horses outside. Brother Frantz came up on horseback with his plump little wife behind him. With them was Brother Schreiber.

"And now what?" exclaimed Sister Landis.

The visitors came in, looking both excited and solemn.

"Take off your things," said Sister Landis hospitably. "And what is it then? No one is hurt? Or sick?"

Sister Frantz looked at her husband.

"A cousin of Brother Schreiber came over from Great Swamp," she began, "and Brother Schreiber came to our place today."

"Well?"

"Brother Duboy is dead," said Brother Schreiber.

"Dead!" cried Sister Landis. "But he was not sick!"

The children gathered around, looking a little frightened, and Anna Elizabeth thought of the kindly blue eyes that had looked at her last September. Was it possible that never again would Brother Duboy sit down beside her and say, "Now you will tell me all about it"? Her father looked both surprised and grieved.

"Sit down now and tell us how it happened," he said.

"Nothing happened," said Brother Schreiber.

"Just got up one morning, he did," said Sister Frantz, taking up the story, "and told the people he was staying with—the Snyders, you know—that he would die that day. And he put on his shroud, and lay down, and he asked them to sing with him, and later that day he died."

Sister Frantz was in tears by the time she had finished her story, and Sister Landis also.

"A good man we have lost," said Brother Landis.

"Very good," said Brother Schreiber, apparently cherishing no unpleasant memories of the Sunday when there had been two sermons.

Still Anna Elizabeth lay still, trying to realize the fact of death. She had been sick, and now she was much better, and would soon be reading her books. Brother Duboy hadn't been sick at all, and yet she was alive, and he was not.

"What did he sing?" asked her mother.

> "Now journey I with gladness,
> To my true fatherland."

And now at last Anna Elizabeth felt the tears come into her eyes. He had started with gladness. Whatever it was that he had been waiting for, he wasn't waiting any more. No longer would he look across autumn fields and say, "The husbandman—waiteth—long."

"Very good it was of you to stop and tell us," said Brother Landis. "When then did he die?"

"March 21," replied Brother Schreiber. "What with the storm and all, we got the news rather late. My cousin brought this package."

"Package?" said Sister Landis.

"It was in his room, the Snyders said, and they thought you would understand. It is for Anna Elizabeth."

A rustle of surprise went round the room.

"Open it then," said Brother Landis, and all the others crowded around to see. Anna Elizabeth lay back in bed wondering what else would happen on her birthday.

"A book!" cried Henry.

"A Bible," said her mother.

"A Halle Bible," added her father. He brought it over to Anna Elizabeth, and she opened it with loving, wondering fingers. On the fly leaf was Abraham Duboy's name written in a hand which she did not know. But under it in his own handwriting was a message:

To the little Anna Elizabeth, for whom there will always be books.

Abraham Duboy.

Again that afternoon Anna Elizabeth found no words to say.

"And why would he be leaving his Bible to Anna Elizabeth?" cried Sister Frantz. It was easy to see that the ride to the Landis home had been a small price for her to pay in order to see for herself what was in the package. "I cannot understand."

"No relatives did he have to leave it to," said Brother Landis thoughtfully.

"And everybody knows that Anna Elizabeth loves books," added Brother Frantz. Anna Elizabeth wondered if he was thinking of the book Michael had brought her.

"Very kind it was of him," said Brother Landis, "and a fortunate girl is Anna Elizabeth. She will keep the Bible carefully, won't you, daughter? It is something to be treasured as well as used."

"Oh, yes, father," said Anna Elizabeth earnestly.

The Bible was going from hands to hands.

"Who wrote his name in, I wonder," said Sister Frantz.

"A great many things about Brother Duboy we never will know," said Brother Landis quietly. "How he could be so alone, and yet so kind and friendly; how he could have seen so much that was unusual and unreasonable in religion and yet have stayed so calm and sensible." There was a pause, and then he repeated the words he had spoken earlier that afternoon. "A good man we have lost."

The visitors got up to leave.

"Anna Elizabeth is better, not?" asked Sister Frantz.

"Much better," replied Anna Elizabeth, speaking for herself. She said her next words a little shyly, for she knew well enough how Sister Frantz felt. "Very nice it was of Michael to give me the book."

Sister Frantz pursed up her mouth. "He *would* do it," she said.

Brother Schreiber looked at the three books on the bed. "And what will you do with all those?" he inquired, shaking his head.

"Read them," said Anna Elizabeth, smiling happily.

"And when will Michael go back?" asked Brother Landis.

"In a day or two," replied Brother Frantz. He turned toward the bed. "You must get well and strong, Anna Elizabeth," he said.

"So I will," she replied, both surprised and pleased.

After the guests were gone and the children were in the other room, Anna Elizabeth's mother gave her more medicine and then told her to lie still and rest. But she left the three books on the bed where Anna Elizabeth could touch them at will.

"Glad I am for my little girl," she said, looking at the books, and Anna Elizabeth smiled at her.

A moment later her father looked in the door. He only smiled too, but Anna Elizabeth knew at least part of what he wanted to say. He touched books with the eager reverence that his daughter knew and imitated. Again Anna Elizabeth smiled. It was very strange, she thought, how something that didn't matter at all you could say as easily as could be, and yet when you really were so happy you didn't think you could stand it, then you couldn't talk at all.

She pushed the pillows aside and snuggled down in bed, content for the time being only to know that she had three books. She, Anna Elizabeth, only thirteen years old, had three books! It was too good to be true, but she could turn her head ever so little and see them lying right beside her. She could feel them if only she moved slightly. There would be time enough to read them later. The grammar, in which easy, ordinary words like *dog* and *cat* and *table* and *chair* had written next to them strange words in an unfamiliar style of printing. Could she ever learn to say those new words that meant the same as the old ones? The *Pilgrim's Progress*, in which she could read for herself the story of Apollyon. The Bible, which had been printed in Germany before she was born, and which Brother Duboy had read for years and years. How long would she have them, she wondered, before she would cease to be surprised when she looked down at them, as she did now?

She thought about Brother Duboy and wondered a little that she did not feel more sorry about his death. She was very sorry indeed to think that she could never talk with him again, but she could not feel sorry for him. She tried to think what heaven was like. She still did not know Revelation so well, but fragments of it were in her mind. "And the books were opened—" That was in Revelation, she was sure. It was like the line from the chapter Brother Kline had read, ". . . and a door was opened in heaven." Heaven must be a place where all sorts of things were opened. Well, if there were books in heaven, they would be good books, and Abraham Duboy would read them, and so it was all right that down on earth in the Oley region, she, Anna Elizabeth, should read the Bible that had been his.

The afternoon sun lay in long yellow patches across

the floor. It was very warm out now after the unusual ice storm. Perhaps Michael would stop in to speak to her before he went back to Germantown to learn more about weaving. The red maple buds would be opening, and he might bring her some, and say, as he had said to her before, "Worth seeing, yes?" She must keep her eyes open to see all the things that Michael saw, and work harder at her spinning and knitting, but always there would be her books to read. She was glad there were books in heaven as well as on earth—one couldn't live long enough to read all he wanted. The patches of sunlight were hazy as she reached out a hand to touch the three books once more. Then she drew a long breath and fell sound asleep, the happiest little girl in all the thirteen colonies.